Umbrella Steps

Julie Goldsmith Gilbert

Umbrella Steps

Random House New York

Manufactured in the United States of America

Remembering E. F.

"May I take one giant step?"
"Simon says no, you may not."
"May I take one umbrella step?"
"Simon says yes, you may take one umbrella step."

Umbrella Steps

My father is giving me away. He is not rejecting me. We both know too much about analysis for that.

When I was younger he used to tell me what bugged him about my mother, so I figured that because he was telling me, wherever she wronged, I didn't. I grew up whole for my father.

One day, the kind of day one does not put a date on, his wife and my mother went mad. Starkers is a choicer word for it, due to the comedy aspects. It was sudden, and right and wrong, and funny and sad. I was there when the head on the body that bore me broke. She was making up this shopping list and she'd listed a whole lot of salad things, the last one being radishes. My mother looked up.

"What comes after R?"

How could I have thought she really wanted to know?

"Mummy, you turned on with the Warbergs last night."

We'd always been very sophisticatedly candid with each other. I thought she'd 'fess up to taking a few tokes with the Warbergs.

"Q comes directly before—what the hell comes after?"

"A. A should do it."

At that point I must have known she wasn't kidding, because she had taken me seriously.

Without having missed a beat, we'd gone from the safe to a shocking thing. One sees those horrors on color TV, while sitting in some cushy den, of women running from flaming places, hair half scorched off, bodies no longer Calgon-soft.

Things ran through my head at that time. I

grabbed them, I do recall, contrary to popular panic. A song from a show about a king. I changed it to queen. "I wonder what the queen is doing tonight? . . . I'll tell you what the queen is doing tonight. She's mad, insane, wacko, barmy—that is what the queen is doing tonight."

My mind right then was playful with famous theatrical mad scenes: Ophelia's, Lady Macbeth's, Blanche DuBois's . . .

And as I watched, like a fool encouraged by the cruel court, she went daffier still. On the scratch pad, beneath radishes, she was writing A-1 Sauce, not once, but over and over. Her mind had turned to shit. I think I must have been embarrassed. I got out of the room. I went to find my father.

What we did with her was correct, I suppose. My father called it "relieving her of . . ." I called it dispossession. She was enrolled in a place outside of Boston. The day she left I took myself to a movie. It was *Persona,* a Bergman film about a woman who just couldn't grasp that she was beyond repair. I think if my mother had seen it, she would have thought, Well, it's the other guy who gets the cancer.

It was the wrong choice of movie, it wasn't an intellectual day. *Muscle Bikini Beach Bango* would have been too heavy for me, but I considered seeing it over again anyhow. Just sitting, calms. I now acknowledge as brothers the people who squeeze in as many movies as their day will hold. I had read an article on this rare breed in *New York* magazine, which tends to cover everything weird in New York (sometimes it has to travel to a borough if the subject is a bit déclassé). In this particular article there were no pictures along with the text. My thought had been that the people were proud, refusing to be photographed, or that the people were unsightly, and the magazine had refused. But it was probably pure shame. There is a depraved feeling that catches a New Yorker if he has fifteen minutes of nothing laid on him.

That day I could have let the Swedish run over me for hours, but when a little snark who resembled Sirhan Sirhan slid his (I hope it was a) briefcase along my calf, I got up.

"You belong in the RKO," I said. I walked out onto Lexington Avenue. It was the RKO. I hadn't even known where I'd been.

I collected the mail and went into the garden. It would have been perfectly macabre to find a letter saying . . . our deepest sympathies upon hearing . . . when nobody knew yet. I'd wanted something sensational to occur, the way it does when someone staid and well-bred, like a political figure, is suddenly booked on charges of extortion.

A fancy store sent a skyrocket bill along with a cool little scented advertisement saying: "If you have anything at all, you'll buy $50.00 worth of navel salve."

Then came the *Turtle Bay Gazette* (lifetime subscription) sporting headlines of "Turtle Bay Turns to Biafra." My sainted mother read this epistle every week. "I like the way they put the news," she would say. A mental note: have *Gazette*'s mailing address transferred to the Snake Pit.

I'd mixed myself a drink, a bullshot . . . sounds as though it might consist of beef enzymes, but a pleasing drink all the same. "Oh feh," says a pixie friend of mine in regards to just about anything. Soooo . . . Feh, I'm a minor in the eyes of New York. I do my drinking at home. I don't rap, groove, or turn my head on. I'm a product of the early fifties and have stayed there. I sleep with older men.

I was sitting there sipping my shot of bull, listening to James Taylor sing about the way it is, babe, a record that my mother had grooved to all last month, when the doorbell rang. Things happen often enough when you're ready for them to do so, but *only* when you don't pray. Praying cancels out everything. In my eighth year I used to compose a thoughtful monologue to Him each night in bed. I'd thought it most humble, when, actually, a dyed-in-the-wool capitalist spoke out. It went:

> *God, thank you for the food, bread, water, clothing, and everything that we have that is good. Most things that we have are good. But listen, ya know that pencil case with the forty-eight all-different-color pencils with magic erasers that Phoebe Kyser got for her birthday? Well, I wouldn't mind if she decided not to love it, God—if she'd hand it over. Please, oh please, don't let me steal it, God. Also, let us have rack of lamb for dinner tomorrow night . . .*

And so it went until I fell asleep, wanting.

It was special delivery flowers from Max Schling at the door. For me. At the established places they always send these pubescent laddies (the son or nephew of) who simply can't take their eyes off your chest (if you're seventeen to twenty-five and braless). This particular "choirboy" looked directly into my eyes, which made me glance down at my chest to see if anything was wrong.

"Flowers for a Miss Prudence Goodrich?"

"Yes, I'm her—she."

"Could you sign here, please?"

"Why? I'm not paying for it."

"Um, could you please sign here?" A polite one (a nephew) working for his tip.

Cocktail party games with delivery boys was a waste of time. "Sure thing—where? On this line?"

"Um, ya, right here—I think."

He placed his finger where I had mine, and they touched. I didn't withdraw—I let him get a finger kick, signed the thing, tipped him well, just to show that I was older than he, and then I was alone again.

In the beginning Nate sent me only flowers because I'd stated that material gifts would make me feel "kept" and forty. But I was a mere sixteen then. Now I know that any woman worth her salt will accept any gift worth its salt. Nate was a good giver. He never thrust, only offered. The only way he knew he wouldn't lose me was to let me go. He was kind and shrewd, but of course he was really up there—forty-five. He'd had time. At my age he would have probably been a smirky hood, passing wind in movie theaters and putting gum in little girls' hair.

We'd known each other for a long time, ever since I was seven, so I'd had the opportunity to watch him develop. If anybody would have told me at age seven that Nate would be in my life at seventeen, I'd have said, "But of course."

Gretel Roerback, Sue Sailigson, BaBa Lattimer, Laverne Washington, and I hung out frequently at Lolly Spitz's house. At thirteen, the things that counted about someone's home were: parents who weren't there much, leftover grown-up party food in the fridge, a secluded roof for smoking, *and* that the person did accurate homework, to be copied by each of us. Lolly Spitz was a winner in all of the categories. Besides, she was a dear girl and my best friend. She was there for my vulnerable times, and at my strongest, she left me alone. Not to make her out a saint, she let me alone because she was envious, but being a true friend, she would never let me know. Lolly was all kinds of positive adjectives—ultimately she was Scarlett O'Hara and I was Melanie Wilkes. She had possessed a figure when it wasn't time yet, lost her virginity at an age when I didn't even know I was masturbating. She kept herself in style before any man ever did.

We would walk down the street and people would look at her. Men and women and even little brat kids. I would watch their faces register longing, searching, personal looks. Street looks are frightfully honest. But for the fact that society forbids it, we'd all walk off with people in the street.

Occasionally Lolly would do her queen-mother routine. If some poor deprived soul really intruded, standing stock-still, openly gaping (the country goof prototype), she would bow her head ever so slightly, cup her hand in a gentle wave, and glide on. Once, surveying the Bowery on a class trip, she demonstrated her royal thing to a wino bum. He would have none of it. Grinning with Roquefort-cheese teeth: "Hey, Queenie, fuck, fuck, fuckie," and he trailed us for blocks, collecting his distinguished colleagues as he went. Quite a following—we literally had the lower depths at our feet. The word had spread and all the torn men stood posted like sentries in every doorway.

"Dance wit da dolly wit da hole in her ha ha."

"I oncet had a daughter looked like you . . . that's why I'm down here."

"Wrap your legs around my neck."

Lolly remained unruffled. She was a hit in any crowd. Every day did something to flatter her. In darkly evil muggy weather, instead of crimping, her hair fell in tendrils. During sieges of wind most blondes are in trouble when their hair flies forward revealing dark roots. Hers was driven straight back, showing only a passionate blond mass.

I asked her, "Why does the wind let you alone?"

"I guess it digs me," she answered.

Every time I was with her someone would comment on her looks, economically side-stepping me to get more of Lolly. I nourished a fantasy. I had to. I was so staggeringly beautiful, see, that only very special people had the proper vision for me. Like a brain ahead of its time, my beauty also had to suffer and wait.

I never failed to approve of and applaud Lolly's luck, but I tried not to go overboard. I felt it my duty to keep her at a mortal level.

In my formative years, we lived at 75th Street, Lolly Spitz lived at 70th Street, and our school lived at 65th. Spanning the ten blocks, Lolly and I went, as a duo, to school each morning. The ritual rarely altered unless we were sick, had trauma, or decided to cut. So every morning during my formative years Nate Spitz saw me with his pants off. I would walk into the unlocked penthouse apartment at eight-thirty, proceed down the hall to Lolly's room, and on the way, at eight thirty-one, would catch Nate Spitz in jockey shorts doing sit-ups in his den.

"Morning, Mr. Spitz."

Neck veins bulging, eyes popping, sweat pouring, he would time it just right.

"Forty-three–hiya, Prude–stick around–forty-four."

I never stuck, because after I passed he would close the door.

I overslept one morning, did everything double

time, and arrived panting at the Spitz's. The door was locked. I rang—nothing. Then I performed one of those irate banging exhibitions. I heard definitely male feet coming. Nate Spitz.

"It's Prudence," I yelled through the still closed door.

"Who asked you?" he bellowed back. When he opened the door, I saw that I'd dragged him out of bed. Pajamas, eight o'clock shadow, piggies in his eye corners—all the evidence.

"Hi, Mr. Spitz—why was the door locked?"

"Hello, Prude—because it's Saturday."

"Oh, is that why I woke you up. I guess I must have mistaken it for a weekday."

Only Nate Spitz would then take a cigarette and lighter out of his pajama pocket. He inhaled deeply. "So you got yourself up and over here just to catch a man in pajamas—cheap thrill, Prude."

On guard, I had thought, on guard with Lolly's father. In fact, for the past year I hadn't been comfortable with Lolly when the subject of "daddy" came up. She had once said, "You know, Daddy thinks that when you lose your baby fat, you'll be a looker."

For the next year I had eaten very little.

That morning I stood before Nate Spitz thin, on my way to being a looker, and he knew it.

"I am accustomed to viewing you in less. Is . . ."

"No, she's not—spent the night on the prowl."

"Well then, when will she get home?"

"I don't know—who shall I say called?"

"The Soledad Brothers—all of 'em."

He took my hand and placed it on his heart. "Prude, you're on your way to being a smart-ass. It does my heart good."

My hand was still under his, on his chest, getting moist.

"Um, Mr. Spitz—when you give me my hand back, there will probably be a stain where it was."

He laughed a lot and dropped my hand. There it was, a hand print on his red silk (Sulka, no doubt) pajama top.

"Do I make you nervous, Prude?"

"Noop," I said, twitching.

"Does your dad get you nervous?"

"No. But it's not the same thing."

Then we had one of those searching-look deals, neither of us breaking for ages. In grade school we used to call it a staring contest, and the one who broke first paid a penalty. After a while I couldn't take it, looked down, and saw a bulge there.

"No, it's not the same," he said finally.

I wished I'd worn zippers instead of buttons. My time had come.

The following Monday, Lolly and I had no classes together. I was relieved. Walking to school with her had been enough of a strain. We usually walked slowly, sometimes stopping for coffee and ciggies, eating each other's words with spoons. But that particular morning there was a generation gap between us.

"Well, tell . . . how was your weekend, Prude?"

"Oh, it was nothing much. I ate a lot."

Lolly was myopic. Sometimes, forgetting that it was an affliction, I had the sensation that her eyes were walking on my brain.

Her mouth crooked up. "Oh yeah . . . what did you eat?"

"Crap. All sorts of crap."

"It doesn't show."

Neither of us was interested in anything other than the unsaid. I replayed the conversation:

"How was your weekend, Prude?"

"I had nookies with Nate Spitz, Lolly Spitz."

"Oh yeah, I know him; he's my father."

"Yes."

"Well, was he any good?"

"Fantas . . ."

"Listen, Prude, I'm stopping at the bookstore. I'll see you at lunch." She turned and walked off. Maybe she knew.

Lolly took her privileges. Although before all this happened with Nate, she had never to my knowledge caught my daddy in his jockey shorts. She's always called him Marvin. "Your mother and Marvin" was the way it went with her.

I was very close to my mother for three days once. Lolly, in her guileless fashion, had seen to it. Electra was put in storage over that particular Abraham Lincoln's birthday. Usually over Washington's or Lincoln's or Columbus's, Lol and I covered the New York movie scene. We'd start at twelve o'clock, noon. By ten o'clock that same night we couldn't remember whether it was John Wayne or Jeanne Moreau who had played the sheriff in the first film.

After several years of sitting on our cans in dark movie houses on great men's birthdays, my mother suggested that we do something healthy. She would emerge at odd times, reminding herself that she had a voice in things. Like an old cuckoo clock.

Actually, mother did keep up with the Jones's, but not with me. She did a consumptive amount of reading dealing with "where to," "when to," and "how to." The "why to's" were left for the more probing readers.

In the winter of '66, the seventy-five-cent magazines declared skiing a must. According to the text, anybody could and should ski, but only in the proper attire, of course. A black family in their warmies, with all the joy in the world, would not have been discovered at the major lodges. They wouldn't even have been allowed to picket.

It was decided. We three would spend the long weekend on the slopes of Mt. Snow. I was puzzled by Marvin's benign approval. Then, at the Spitz's house, while dabbling through a leading men's magazine, I saw the angle. I had turned to a color spread of a folksy ski resort in Vermont. The article featured the numerous activities provided for *après le ski.* Nothing about how to get a ski boot on or what to do once it's on. What *is* a herringbone? No matter. What is a "snow bunny"? Ah, now that's more to the point. Snow bunnies are pretty girls who sex-twitch around the slopes, never intending to ski. They are amateur decoys posted to divert male skiers with professional intent. With a new socio-libido slant, the rugged sport had suddenly become appetizing to Marvin Goodrich in that year of our debauched Lord.

My father would not be sharing the rope tow

with my mother. He would not be sharing her bed or her needs. He was going to act out something I had read about in a magazine.

I was packing. I kept unpacking to check how I looked in the clothes I was packing. How did I look? A grandmotherly comment on me would have been "You look very nice, dear," which is tantamount to saying "You look like a dish of vanilla ice cream." Once this applicant for a blind date asked me how I looked. I said, "Like a discount."

I stopped being "all the way with JFK" when he initiated his physical fitness program. I've always wished to move as little as possible, and he intruded on my bodily privacy. Not everyone is built like a Kennedy and carries a guest racquet in the trunk of the caaa. I used to think (as a child leaping into galaxies) that I was born without muscle tone, a dystrophy of some sort, and that any day "They" would inform me. It would have guaranteed a standing excuse from gym, and I would have gotten all hollow-looking—like a "Kean child" painting—and would have been placed on the nourishment list at Camp Renoruck. But my leg always went flying when the good doctor gave me the knee bang, nobody broke anything gently to me, and I continued to be chosen last on teams in gym class.

I put on my new sparkling-white parka. I looked like a stuffed cabbage. Why couldn't people see me the way I saw myself in my mind's eyes? Or at least have the courtesy to say that I resembled my mother? I would had gladly taken over her fading beauty, but no free rides for me. I had my own set of no looks. Outstanding feature: shoulders. My bottom has a charming dimple in it, but that's an attribute I could never quite play on. Sans shoulders and dimple, I was still only able to see how I didn't want to appear.

A note was slipped under my closed door. My mother did this frequently. There was a certain lack of direct contact between us. Maybe she thought I was busy performing unnatural acts that required uninterrupted concentration. It was on her personal stationery, sealed, my full named printed on the envelope. This type of formality was one of the "niceties" that made up for her life. Her handwriting looked like ant doody.

Dear Prudence—

I don't want to disturb you, dear. I know that you're busy packing and what not. I had a lightbulb. Why don't you ask one of your friends to join us on our petit vacance? It's up to you, but I think it would be nice. Short notice, I know, but it didn't occur to me until now. Tell whoever you decide on that she should dress accordingly. Please, dear, not Laverne Washington. She makes me quite nervous.

Love—Mummy

With only a day's notice, Lolly managed to become a ski bunny.

Her bill to Mr. Nate Spitz:

1 parka, rabbit-fur-lined—$55.00
2 prs. ski pants—$80.00
1 pr. lounge pajamas—$40.00
1 pr. goggles—$10.00
Love—Abercrombie & Fitch

Both my mother and I were athletes of the mind. We talked a good game but couldn't play one. Intent is not a simile for prowess. We were not meant to ski, and because of our shared disability, we formed a tentative alliance. Marvin and Lolly made up the opposition. With perfect snowplows and snow-burned cheeks, they chair-lifted into the sunset. Pals.

"Good for Lolly!" Mother said as we waved them off at the rope tow on the second morning. I wasn't as charitable.

"Show-offs usually break something, you know . . . I'm surprised her boobies don't get in her way."

Mother sat down in the snow. "They seldom do," she whispered. It was the only time she'd really been stylish.

The beginners' class met after lunch. Part one of our lesson was "Learning How to Fall," which on a full stomach had to be very European. Eat a little something, then we see what we can do. Ya?

As the afternoon got longer, our instructor became more Teutonic. Clipping his sentences. Gesturing only when necessary. "Zip, zip. Bend zee knees! You von't die!"

He called himself Rolf Wolfkrank. He was cosmetically handsome. I felt that a better ash-blond hair dye would have been smarter. Perhaps even a tooth bleach to flash up his smile. Minor details. Perfection is an art, but so is detection.

He did his job. He saw to it that the flabby ladies in their ill-fitting custom snowsuits got their husbands' money's worth. He'd made himself into someone they could talk about over canasta hands:

"Dolly, he actually held me when I fell. Very foreign!"

Ya! . . . Ha! . . . Ralphie Wolff probably cowered inside his lederhosen that someday someone from his hometown of Teaneck, New Jersey, would appear on his slope . . .

The sun set; Mummy's rib broke. She'd learned how to fall too hard. Lolly and Marvin hadn't checked back all day, and so, with mild irritation, I inherited the dutiful-daughter role. Luckily, the place where we'd been skiing was leveled off, making it easier to half walk, half carry her to the first-aid hut. She bore up rather well, crying for the correct amount of time and then chatting madly to divert herself from the pain.

"I should have gone to Florida."

"You hate Florida."

"Yes, I suppose I do. The women are so dreadful there. They wear gold mules and make their husbands carry their handbags. Certain parts are beautiful though. The Keys—that would have been nice . . ."

"Well, you should have said something. If Daddy was agreeable to this, he would have gone along with anything."

She had shifted her weight, making me strain to support her. I sent evil thoughts to my father. Her eyes filled. Not from rib pain. "Anything young and pretty. Prudence, I need your dark glasses."

I slipped them on over her tears. "You're pretty . . . and almost young. Our instructor kept giving you the old rogue eye."

A male attendant in white was walking toward us. Mother got in her last licks: she must have been smiling. "For heaven's sake, Prudence! You can't mean that silly mama's boy from . . . Bayside!"

"You noticed."

"Oh, I notice a lot of things."

That was special. But of course, Mummy and I, we would never be friends.

When the vagabonds got back, Mother was propped up in bed, sipping mulled wine and looking ragged around her edges. I had been stoking the fire, trying to make things agreeable for her. The lodge was rrrrustic: no upstairs maids to turn down beds or bring breakfast trays with roses on them.

They entered her bedroom with flaming cheeks, tired but happy travelers.

"What's this?" Daddy asked, not caring.

"Is something wrong?" Lolly, with the shining eyes.

I acted as interpreter. They both gave little mews of sympathy. They explained their delay, which lacked detail. A nasty accident on one of the high slopes. A child with a broken body. They had stayed to help.

Then they left to catch dinner before the dining room closed.

I went to bed early, hoping that I was tired. I lay

there wall-eyed. It angered me the way Lolly had barged into my mother's bedroom. She certainly took her privileges.

I woke up to Lolly's deserted bed and a note:

Prudie—

The best skiing is early skiing. Will be back for lunch.

Luv—Lol

I recruited a couple of strangers, who helped me get my mother down to breakfast. The doctor had bound mother's rib cage tightly in order to prevent the fractured rib from floating around. It caused her to move in a disjointed way, the body walking behind the head. People in the dining room stared at her and I kept wishing that she'd stayed in bed. She looked palsied.

When her soft-boiled eggs came and when she finally got the spoon to her mouth, she then made an ugh face like an absolute toddler.

"Not to your liking, Mother?"

"They're so runny."

I tasted the eggs. "Same as usual. Just the way you like them."

Her damn eyes filled up again. "They probably are. I didn't seem to get much sleep."

"Why?"

Soft-boiled eggs with a side of tears . . . "Oh, I don't know. I just felt lonely."

Lolly did come back early, like a good girl should. . . . I had refused to have any more thoughts on the matter.

"I bet they did it on the rope tow," I said, on the couch many moons later. "Probably gave each other a little feel on the chair lift for starters, although that would be awfully plebeian of Daddy."

Then I whipped around to search the imperturbable face of my conscience. "Ah ha! Caught ya. Is eating your breakfast a substitute for ingesting my problems?"

The doctor buttered the horn of his croissant while meeting my gaze with the third eye of Freud. Mute was the masticator.

"Listen, you know it's very rude to talk while eating," I mocked him.

The thing he'd taught me was to allow niggling points to irritate me to a tantrum level, whereupon, screaming like a banshee, I'd drop about ten years. Then, seeing that I was totally dependent, he would say flatly, "In our next hour we'll pick this up again," leaving me, thumb in mouth, waiting for someone to slip me a breast.

He gave his raspberries a dollup of Devonshire cream. I was in control.

"I'm paying for that *bon repas*, ya know . . ."

He continued scooping his food in silence. My hate bubbles were starting, I felt like a pressure cooker. I wondered if there was an "Anna Freud," and if there was, where in the hell she bought Devonshire cream. Probably smuggled it out of the conference in Vienna.

"There you sit like Little Miss Muffet eating her turds and way. Then along came a spider and . . ."

I needed to be physical. I'd lost control. Reacting over, I grabbed a fist of berries and waited for a reaction. His spoon was poised over the berry dish. Three remained. He ate them calmly, his expression inscrutable, his third eye filming my display. Psychiatrists have the power to drive you crazier than any relationship on the outside.

"Now what do I do?" I yelled.

He dabbed his mouth with a damask napkin (no Scotkins for a forty-dollar-an-hour man).

"May I suggest you lie down."

"What'll I do with these?" The raspberry juice had begun to trickle down my wrist.

"Why don't you eat them?"

"Don't want to," I snapped.

"Then why did you take them?"

"That's for me to know and you to find out."

"I'm trying," he said, very earnest, reminding me of a TV commercial I'd seen where this young counselor is soft-selling a camp for autistic children. How to get through to kids who defeat medical science? Keep trying! With strains in the background of Peter, Paul & Mary singing "I'm on my way."

I released the berries back into the bowl, smiling as he offered me his napkin and some Kleenex. "Why? Am I that messy?"

He brushed his mod tie of invisible crumbs and recrossed his legs. "The napkin's for your hand. The Kleenex in case of spillage."

I felt scalp prickles. "What are you getting at?"

"It's you, I believe, who is about to get at some pretty raw material. We both know it's easier if you lie down."

He had created an element of suspense. It was as though there was a third person in the room, the monster inside of me. If I would only lie down, the two of us could conjure her up. I lowered myself. "Okay, I'm ready for the unveiling. But wait—you want to know a truth? I always think that you get me prone just so you can be free to jerk off, or pick your nose, or sneak candy."

He took a while to answer, which seemed testament to the fact that he was doing one of those very things. "You seem to be preoccupied with people acting behind your back." His tone was medicinal.

Mine was hostile: "I refuse to understand you!" There was a warmth in my hair. The spillage had started. I waited to be led.

"Do you remember what you were talking about when you grabbed my berries?"

"Yes. Daddy and Lolly. And their having a thing behind my back in the snow."

It was his turn. He used his brushed voice because he knew he'd hit on something juicy and didn't want to spoil it. "Why did you grab, Prudence?"

Soft, soft, but that big stick was going to git me. "I don't know. I . . . wanted something . . . that was *mine* to touch, I guess."

"Could it be . . ." The Doc was really sneaking up on me, a paid assassin. "Could it be that you wanted to grab your father's penis away from Lolly?"

I had a flash daydream: a huge audience was on its feet, stomping, cheering, whistling and applauding. I stood up, lurching my body as if to get rid of it. "I hate you! My hour is up and I absolutely hate you!"

Actually, the doctor looked sallow. The food on his breakfast tray had gone practically uneaten.

"Am I right?" he asked, walking me to the door.

He'd earned his money.

"Probably," I said.

Thank God, I had a private phone. Few ears can resist extensions. I didn't like putting my people through the business of talking to my mother.

"Hello, Mrs. Goodrich . . . um . . . how are you?"

"I'm just fine, dear, thank you. How are you?"

"Fine. Um . . . could I please speak to Prude?"

"Who shall I say is calling?"

"Oh, this is Laverne."

"Oh, well, hello, Laverne, how are you?"

"I'm fine, thank you, Mrs. Goodrich, how are you?"

So when the Princess phone came on the market, I asked for it, as any respectable Jewish or Protestant princess would.

My mother said, "Two phones in one house is one too many phones. You're not that popular."

My father said, "Give me a rough estimate on the number of guys that call you a week."

"About two hundred."

"In that case, I suppose your business depends on a phone."

Done.

That Monday night Nate called me. "Hiya, Prude, how's your ass?"

"Hello, Mr. Spitz, clean, thank you."

"If you keep calling me mister, I'll have to hire you as a secretary."

"That would be fine. I'd sit cross-legged on your desk, with no panties on."

"Dictation would be suspended immediately. The business would fall apart. You'd ruin me. We'd be forced to apply for welfare."

"And all because of Carter's underpants with an elastic top."

"We've got to talk about that, Prude—got to get you some indecent underwear."

"There's a place on 42nd Street and Broadway. They specialize in obscene stuff. I'm sure you know it well."

There was a pause. Nate decided to break the trend of conversation. He knew when to become Mr. Spitz again. "I only know the class stores, Puss. On Saturday we'll go to one of the better stores and get you some panties."

I chanced it. "Yes, Daddy," I said.

About fifteen minutes later Lolly called me. "Who have you been gabbing with for so long?"

"Hi, Lol, me personal life is me own."

"Well, all I can say is that if you're going to have privates, I'll have to shop for another confidante."

I knew she was kidding, but kidding is always half of something else. "I was talking to one of my men, if you must know."

"José from Gristede's, or Frank from the cleaner's?"

It was time for it. We didn't go to a progressive school for nothing. She'd fed me the bait. She was my best friend. She had to know so that I could discuss it with her.

"Neither. It was Nate from the Spitz's."

Although I knew Lolly completely, this had to be one of her danger areas. I couldn't predict her reaction. I didn't want to breathe until she said something.

"Well, say something."

"Something."

Oh Jesus, she wasn't with me. Phone silences are deadly. The longer you wait, the less you have to say. I wanted to replace the receiver quietly, the way "breathers" do. Also, I was scared. Someone had once advised me "Never lose a friend over a man." But wise advice never quite handles the extenuating circumstances like "never lose a friend over a man who happens to be the father of the friend."

"Lol?"

"Yes?"

"Well . . . at least you won't want to steal him."

Two feet, with shoes on, right in the mouth. That's never been one of my fortes—smoothing things over. I usually end up saying "Listen, I love you" and hope it will serve. The receiver was wet with hand juice. Love is so close to hate, it's incredible. She must have been feeling the latter when she spoke.

"I don't have to steal him, Prudence. The reason this is happening at all is because he really wants me. Consider yourself an understudy."

Now, there was nothing that I could have taken the wrong way about that statement. It was a zinger and she'd meant to hurt me. Strangely, I wasn't hurt. I knew Lolly had done time with her analyst, though I hadn't really known the part of her that needed help. Only once had she mentioned her mother's death. "Nobody can ever hurt me again," she'd said. But her bitch reaction to my "state of affairs" was out of character and peculiar. I thought she'd have a giggle with it after she'd digested.

"Listen, Prudence, I have to hang up. When my head gets to a place where I think you and Daddy are a gas, we'll be together again. In the meantime, I'd rather not know you."

I had homework to do, dinner to eat, hair to wash, and something to cry about.

In our sophomore year, there were other key men in our life. Namely, Stanton Aurbach: a former oceanographer who'd lost some toes (which we hadn't the foggiest, until at a school picnic when he took off his shoes and there wasn't much left on his feet, and we were all terribly sad and terribly nauseated). He taught sophomore chemistry. Odd choice. One explosion and his fingers would have gone the way of his toes. Ugh, and no fingers could be spotted, though I suppose a man with constant gloves on would create a certain mystique. He'd probably considered the odds. I think he was a very serious masochist.

But with his well-crafted Italian leather orthopedic shoes on, he had a musty Old World sex appeal. We all developed longings for him, with the exception of Laverne Washington, who had a goodly portion of Negro blood in her, which made her restrain from messing with whitey. Premature "groupies" was what we were. Sucking up and browning and "Oh wow, Mr. Aurbach, do you mean that H_2O is reeeeely water?" It was all innocence—organized attempts at seduction, little geishas with nothing to offer but giggles. No thoughts of going down on Mr. Aurbach just for a B+. Besides, you couldn't get to him. So aloof. It was as though he occasionally dropped by, a movie star visiting a neighboring lot. He never even signed excuses from chem class. He really didn't fit into our permissive school system and we loved him for it. Ultra-modern should be an anagram for antiseptic. Aurbach physically wore tradition; it made him sexy.

In the seed-pearl school we went to, we were supposed to know the staff not as people upon whom our college educations almost solely depended, but as chums. The yearbook photographer probably did indeed make a little book, snapping the most intimate of "candids." Last year BaBa Lattimer, pictured head to head, arms grazing, with Mme. Devreaux, who had dumped a fat D– on BaBa the preceding semester. The caption, even more of a blasphemy: "Earnest pupil with overzealous faculty member." Now Mme. Devreaux was not in the least masculine, but the plant was there.

Anyhow, in a gross attempt at familiarity amongst the "aristocracy," I found out a few things. Mr. Aurbach was going to have a birthday. Nobody knew when, but he had to have one. In a class meeting the subject was brought up, discussed, nominated, voted, and passed by a minor majority. A gift for Mr. Aurbach. See Mr. Aurbach smile, oh! Look! See Mr. Aurbach get toasty warm. One of Lolly's followers was appointed to find out his date of birth and, if possible, the hour. No one cared to know the year. Lolly and I were elected as Shopper and Shopper's Assistant—Lolly because she had the best taste; I, because I was her best friend. No, to be perfectly smug, my election was testimony to the fact that I had engaged in the only known living conversation of any length with our subject, Aurbach.

So help me. For once the shadow had a flesh-and-blood event all to herself. Lolly took it hard. Stanton Aurbach launched me on the map.

The school library was not a room that I took lightly. I was monastic in that place—nix on spitballs, note passing, and suppressed hee-haws. Not that I received the wine and the wafer before entering, but it was the closest I could relate to a Holy House. It was also the best free bookstore in town. Nothing was banned. If the book had a publisher, our library stocked it. They also carried magazines for all ages, of all interests. So you got half a cigar store thrown into the bargain. I spent most of my idleness there, when Lolly wasn't convenient (when I could get away from Lolly). (Wash my mouth.)

Tuesdays and Thursdays, ten A.M. to twelve

noon, Lolly had chemistry. The library had me, which really wasn't fair because I was in a pleasure dome while she was in a test tube.

It was a Tuesday. I had an English assignment due on that Friday a week, and those dividend four hours of research would bring me a good paper. *Crime and Punishment* had been the reading assignment. The written part was to pick one character and give a detailed analysis on how that character's life served the book in a technical sense, and how his being there affected the other characters emotionally and psychologically. Part I (b) was to summarize (in depth) the entire book and how it might have read, *minus* your chosen character. Part II consisted of pretending to be your character for one contemporary day, walking in his shoes, seeing with his eyes, dealing with alien American life. Part II (b) (if ya made it through the night) was to script an imaginary free-form dialogue between you and your character. Sophomore English, she was a bitch! Part III should have been to translate the whole book back into the original Russian.

I had selected to investigate Svidrigailov, the weirdo friend of Raskolnikov, who commits suicide. The best suicide I've ever read. I was mucking around the Russian section, finding nothing useful, when I spotted Mr. Aurbach squatting in the Italians. Nothing unusual about seeing a teacher, but he did happen to have a class at that time.

Honor the silence of thy library. I couldn't help it. "*Pssst,* Mr. Aurbach . . ." Everyone looks up at a *pssst* in a library. He didn't. With a motivation that startled me, I sidled into Italian territory, squatting beside him. I cleared my corny throat. He knew someone was almost sitting on him—didn't want to get involved. I tried to left-cut which works for some people. "Why, Mr. Aurbach, fancy meeting you here."

His eyes remained straight ahead. The body altered, recoiled. "Your tone sounds menacing, Prudence."

Ship to shore, he read me!

He moved his head around slowly, as it at gunpoint ("One move and I'll blow yer f'in' brains out").

Pupils: dilated; whites: jaundiced.

Then, I didn't know the signs of the weed. But even to me, it was pretty obvious that Aurbach was stoned out of his f'in' mind. Later I realized that he probably turned on a lot because of his toes.

"What are you doing here?" I asked, almost adding, "I won't tell." Too sanctimonious.

"I'm happy here," he said simply.

There are two kinds of murmuring, intimate conversations—bed and the library. Our bodies were close, our hands touching books we didn't see.

"Why did you cut your class, Mr. Aurbach?"

"Because I knew I'd hate them today, Miss Goodrich."

There was nothing left after such a straight answer. A round peg in a round hole. No groping, very satisfactory. *Commedia dell'Arte F307.* I was looking at a book that had been listed as lost when I'd needed it the month before. "I'm happy here too," I offered.

He ran a thin hand through thick hair. His attention could have been anywhere. I wanted to take his temperature. "Tell me, are you two related?"

Zing. He meant Lolly. "Above the skin," I said.

"The best way," he answered.

I tried being brittle. "How so?"

Even with his speech slightly slurred, I was no match for him. "Surgically speaking," he said, accompanied by a foxy glance.

I half got the implication, but as a reflex I said, "What?!?" anyway. My look must have avowed that I am my brother's keeper, and I am! I am!

He kept me threaded. "Local anesthetic. The growth is cut off. Stitches. Healing. Nine out of ten, it doesn't grow back."

He was hurting me. I looked away, hoping,

crazily, that he wouldn't touch me. Russia was safer. "Don't you like Lolly?" I plead for my peace of mind.

He weighed this and then grinned endearingly. "Chemically, yes. Psychologically, no."

"You're crazy! You think she's crazy!" He would flunk me for sure when he came to and remembered our tête-à-tête.

His hand combed his hair again. No wonder it always looked dirty at the end of the day. "Lolly Spitz is complicated for others and simple to herself," he said in summation.

He got up suddenly, throwing himself off balance. One of us reached out. Our hands locked, helping each other to our feet. I needed a parting sentence, something double-edged. Involuntarily: "I don't feel so well, Mr. Aurbach."

He laughed. The library people looked at us. Leaning down, tender: "And I feel better, Miss Goodrich."

The birthday researcher didn't come through, but with defiance: "Tough titty Lolly, there are no records of his birth!"

Lolly was being huffy, but understandably so. The collection had been taken, the gift stylishly purchased—a black canvas director's chair with "Stan Baby" embossed in gold on the back—and then, no day to give it on. Having an inside track on "Stan Baby," I suggested that we give it on a rainy day and hope for the best. Lolly objected, saying that she could have tackled the job by merely placing a three A.M. phone call, thereby jolting him into a confession.

I raised my hand. "Dirty dealing, Lolly."

She retorted out of order. "They say it's the only way to get ahead in this world, Prudie." Our horns locked. Bryan versus Darrow. She was voted down. With red guilt I nominated her as the giver. All said aye, returning her to favor.

She got rid of the bloody thing the next day. With her innate sense of drama, she'd arranged herself around the gift. Her body was bathed in black, matching the canvas. Her hair, a bit more golden than the day before, pinpointed the initials. Special effects always.

Several of us huddled outside as she went into the lab where he took his coffee (or grass) break. Lolly took her sweet time in there.

Laverne Washington said, "They're necking."

I said, irritated, and worried that they were, "I certainly hope not. The gift's not *that* hot."

BaBa "Goosey Lucy" Lattimer: "But Lolly is."

She came out like a stunt woman—flying and

somersaulting. Fire-eating. Wrapping me up as she raced down the hall to the bathroom. I'd known in advance that something quite terrible would happen. She never moved like that; her body was dialed to legato.

"Lol?"

She'd locked herself in one of the cubicles. "Go way."

"You carried me in here . . . so here I stay."

I waited for a half hour while she went through agonized, smothered screams and gaggings. In order to avoid giving her away to anyone who might come in, I went into the cubicle beside her. I hated to monopolize another toilet but I supposed that eventually I'd feel the call to tinkle.

Finally she unlocked the door. I unlocked mine. No words. I watched her watch herself in the mirror. I felt like a hand-held camera on someone coming out of an ordeal. She was acting again, for me, for herself. Before she'd been a real girl having a real hurt at being rejected. It had been healthier. She combed her hair. She carefully redid her shattered face. She pinched her cheeks, reviving the color that had been taken away by Mr. Aurbach's honesty. Call it prophetic. I knew that she'd made a pass at him in that room.

She turned, smiling brightly, ready to be herself again. "Prudie?"

She was willing to let it go. By tomorrow, done up in her apricot suede, it would mean nothing. But when she was thirty it would show up again in her eyes, or have left its mark on her chin or forehead. I decided to trespass. I had to be careful—to talk turkey was to trap a butterfly. "How awful can it be, Lol?"

She dug into her make-up kit again. Lip gloss the final touch to forgetting. But her eyes flickered aware; her voice rippled metallic: "Don't pry, my pet, it doesn't suit you."

I met her evenly in the mirror. "Neither does being avoided," I said.

A month before, she would have linked her arm through mine, saying, "I prithee, coz, be merry"—a line from *As You Like It,* which we had produced in Theater Club our freshman year. She, Rosalind the bold; I, Celia, the meek. A great deal of Lolly's influence over me was in charmingly re-creating memories. I've never met anyone who, like a storybook lover, could allow the present to recede so effortlessly.

But something feline had slithered in between us. I don't know when and I don't know why, but it was a relief. Watching her that day, it occurred to me for the first time that I might be grateful that I was nothing remotely like her.

The next move Lolly made gave me a view of a checklist of violent emotions. She hoisted an insolent bottom up on the sink ledge, crossed a leg, and said, as blasé as a cow depositing, "Got any cake mascara, Prude?"

Everybody has her own language of desperation; that was hers. Even so, I hit the fan: "No. But boy, I wish I did, so you could make your eyes kohl-black and really look like the teacher's pet tart! You need the kind that you have to spit on so you can spit things out. You never do, you just hoard it all up like some kind of dance-hall girl stuffing dollars down her bosom. You're on your way to being a fake, Lolly."

My sermon had reached her pew. Lolly's tears were tracking through her Blush-on. I'd never seen her cry, except once, in a movie, where Deborah Kerr got crippled and couldn't meet Cary Grant at the top of the Empire State Building. Equation: if I could make Lolly sob for herself instead of some celluloid heroine, I was worthwhile having as a friend.

She rocked herself until I went to her and supplied my chest. Holding her while she wet my front, I tried a bit of levity: "Pretend it's the broad kind and pound your fists if you want." She seemed to enjoy the letting go, and yipped for a long time. Finally I put wet dispenser toweling on her eyes so that she wouldn't resent me when they puffed up.

Then, through the burping and heaving of mild hysteria, she told what Aurbach had done to her. She'd knocked, and hearing a muffled acknowledgment, had entered the room to find him sucking air. I stopped her: "What are you talking about?" She dismissed it, saying that he seemed to be out of breath.

"Okay, okay. So go on!" I said, impatient with her naïve details.

Apparently he had given her the admiring once-over and then turned on her, saying cryptically that the funeral reception was down the hall.

"Lolly, that's funny," I said, wiping away her newest tear.

She grabbed my hand. "It's not, it's treacherous. But wait till you hear what else."

"Well, you better hurry. I have a class."

In a rush not to lose her listener, she told me how she'd presented the gift, how he'd seemed pleased, and how, when she'd asked "How pleased, Mr. Aurbach?" he'd grabbed her.

I once had a class to go to. "You mean he kissed you?"

"More," she said vehemently. "He started to make

out, and he was really getting into it, with the heavy breath and all, and he was *really* good." Her green eyes widened into orgasm.

"Go on," I commanded like a hypnotist.

"Well, after he'd been using his tongue for a while and getting all hard and everything, and making my body feel like running water, he suddenly sort of jackknifed and shoved me away."

"And?" I ordered.

"And," she said, picking up the beat, "then he called me a C.T., which I think means something horrid, and then he said, 'I'd tell you to get to a nunnery, but you don't have the class of an Ophelia,' and then —Oh, Prudence, he cut the chair!"

It was too much for comedy. "Lolly, nobody does that."

But if truth gives you the shakes, she was telling it. "He did! He did. I saw him! He took that big scissors that we used to cut the dissected frog's tendons with and he wrecked the chair. Then I ran before he could use them on me."

I slid to the floor. "Jesus H. Christ," I said.

"Stanton L. Aurbach," she said, starting to giggle.

"What's the L?"

"Loon." And the giggle became laughter, peals of it.

We both broke up, clearing the air like disinfectant. Guffawing and shrieking and bellowing in the soundproof bathroom.

"Bet you don't know what the Q in Robert Q. Lewis stands for," I gasped.

Wiping away a good tear, she held her side. "What?"

"Probably Quiggle." I exploded gleefully. We were both rocking around with our sore stomachs, joyous that we'd pulled each other through. "Lolly, I just wet my pants."

"Spread your legs, they'll dry faster." And we launched into new laugh heights. She sobered first. "You know who Mr. Aurbach reminds me of?"

"Who?" I wasn't ready yet.

"That Russian guy you wrote your paper on."

"Svidrigailov?"

"Right. The one who killed himself."

A chair cutter. Not funny. I stopped laughing.

A sexual involvement with a much older man should be a requisite for all seventeen-year-old girlies. And not strictly for the shock value, because if that continues too long, it can prevent the intimate, total involvement from happening. But you have to become your own best friend. Nobody in the "guard" sponsors that sort of thing.

Lolita and I, we would have been friends.

The next time—after that first Saturday morning in his apartment—that I went to bed (sophomore term habit) with Nate, it was on the floor of his office. I had gotten excused from school early in order to finish a paper on "The Dynamics of the Relationships between Nathaniel Hawthorne and His Fictional Women." I had concentrated heavily on Hester Pryne, believing her to be the consummate woman in Nate Hawthorne's life. She's a strange, almost dislikable heroine, but she got to me. Odd ducks always do. I typed up the final page and needed to show off my masterpiece to somebody. The house was empty except for Selma, who was in the kitchen reading *Soul on Ice* in between breading the chicken. She had Panther tendencies lurking and would mentally spit on my neat white papers. I really wanted to read it to Lolly, so I did the next best thing.

"Nate Spitz, please."

"Who shall I say is on the line?"

This one sounded like an Elaine May takeoff. She was cracking her gum madly. She probably used Streaks 'n' Tips on her hair, and wore a 42¢ black, heavily boned brassiere.

"Just tell him that Hester Pryne wishes to speak with him."

"He's on another line right now. Will you hold?"

These broads never wait for an answer. They just zap you right into a vacuum. Phone power, Jesus. Can you imagine calling one of those "Help your favorite suicide" places and being put on hold?

Finally she decided to release me, and then, of course, she had to ask me who I was again. It's not difficult to develop a loathing for a phone voice.

"Jesus! Hester cunt you Pryne."

She giggled. "A little more work on those come-backs, hon. The line's clear now."

"Hiya, Hester, how's your ass?"

"Listen, I have a great hate for your secretary."

"You're supposed to."

"Don't program me. It reflects. It reflects on the entire office, you know. She's got no class and I bet her underwear's dirty."

"Hey, hey—take it easy, Puss." His voice sounded parental. But how else could he sound? I'd been close to a tantrum. How disappointing for both of us.

I thought I'd read enough Françoise Sagan to carry the whole thing off. Actually, the only other men in my experience of immaculate virginity had been a junior from Horace Mann, the grandson of some old friends of my grandmother's, who brought me a camellia corsage that died immediately on my dress. And Ronnie Sapper, a boy I went to camp with, who felt me up during a potato-sack race.

"The reason I called was not to hate anybody but to read you a brilliant paper I just finished."

"I must confess that I dislike being read to, especially over the phone, and especially by a lady with tears in her gullet."

His voice was soft and he'd called me "lady." What a kind term that is, for someone who feels more like a child.

"Prude?"

"What?"

"I want to read your paper. In fact, I want to read it pronto. So you take a cab and bring it over here. I'll read it and then we'll discuss it. Does that appeal to you?"

"Very much. But I can't take a cab. I have no bread."

"None of your lip. Write a check. I'll see you in twenty."

I changed my clothes four times, and then had trouble with my diaphragm. Way back when I got it, I had asked the nurse to show me exactly how to insert it, but she'd seemed to find that distasteful and gave me a blueprint. In rehearsing I always got caught on step number 2.

My mother made my puberty decision. "You've reached it," she said the day after my thirteenth birthday. "Let's celebrate."

It took me a while to figure out how she knew I'd gotten the "voofs." It must have been the sheet that I'd bled on in the middle of the night, vowing to change it come morning. I'd forgotten Selma had apparently discovered my new ability to be a woman and had presented the evidence to the reigning woman of the house. The fact that Mother had come upon the knowledge in such a roundabout way made me feel more of a child, one who leaves messes.

Our whoopee celebration one week later included a trip to the gynecologist, with cinnamon toast at Rumpelmayer's as a chaser. My mother looked muted and chic in brown and beige. Since we rarely did things in tandem, she'd made an effort to appear unified. Usually I caught her before she could present herself to me. On the rare morning when she pried herself up to see me off to school, she'd be wearing a brilliantly colored geometric hostess gown, with a totally helpless face on top.

When I was very wee, things must have been

going smoothly inside of her. She was beautiful. Except for the patch which destroyed her face when I was five, and from then on, it was downhill.

The details are not accurate, but the sight memory is still with me. It had been raining the icy streets of February. A lady named Grace, who'd been our token colored "friend" at the time, had called for me at kindergarten. I think I donated a lot of love to her; she could make hot cereal without any lumps. (Black kids' mothers have a marvelous feel for white people's neurotic kids.) While putting on my galoshes, she warned me about the patch. My mother, who was a model, had been working in an exclusive designer's showroom, and for one of the evening outfits her eyelids had been studded with sequins. One had slid down into her eye. She'd been whisked away by some courier to Manhattan Eye, Ear and Throat Hospital, where, after undergoing minor surgery, she was whisked home to lie on her chaise longue and wait for my reaction. I remember the panic upon hearing about a no longer normal mommy. I screamed at Grace, "No, I don't want her! I won't go back home. She's a witch now!" And Grace, with her soft, hymnal cadence, doing up my leggings: "Now, honey, she may be hurt, but she ain't nothin' bad like that."

I went home with Grace and was promptly fed

something similar to a dog yum-yum to placate me before going in to pay my respects to The Patch.

The drapes were closed and I couldn't make out much on account of the great boulder which was Grace's backside. Buzzing with fear and loving it, I allowed one peek and saw her face. I behaved in accordance with what I thought I'd seen. Moaning, I yanked at Grace's clothes, jerking my head toward the door ("Let's beat it, Tonto, Scarface is coming"). Within the limits of my peek in a dim light, I'd noticed not the patch itself, but the thin black band running diagonally across her cheek, holding the patch in place. Then mother held out her hand. It dangled limply from her wrist. She cooed at me, "Come here, Prudie. Come here, lovey. Come." No go. Even is she'd offered candy or a new Madame Alexandre doll with a full wardrobe, it wouldn't have worked. I bolted from the room. No excuses about being a mere child. I knew how I should have reacted. I should have (kissed the ring of the withered old Pope and genuflected), but I didn't. I repent.

Years later, on the day of my diaphragm fitting, she looked to me the way it had been before the patch. In the waiting room we didn't talk, but she'd glance up from her magazine and smile like she was taking the right steps for her daughter and all. The other two women in the room were both competent with pregnancy. They watched us. Mother with her smart mink beret and flat waistline; me with my shrubs of acne and penny loafers. They probably wondered who was going in for what.

"Likewise" the doctor and nurse. After a hasty back-of-the-hand conference, I was ushered into his trophy-lined office (. . . and in 1956 awarded to the man who gives the best feel under the Hypocritical oath). He was young and dippy instead of old and kindly. His hair was water-slicked and he shot me a smile full of dollar signs. "Personally," he said, not looking at me, "I feel that you're a bit premature for this type of examination." I sat upright in his oily leather "relax" chair. He'd implied that my mother had poor judgment, which was correct. She did. But my protective instincts at that moment were more correct. "I'm sure that my mother knows what she's doing. You *seem* to come very highly recommended." I gave him my best eyebrow arch, trying to suggest that it was he who had the lousy judgment.

The nurse appeared on cue. "Nurse," he said, "you can prepare Miss Goodrich."

Cinnamon toast dripping with butter, hot chocolate so rich that it weighed in the cup, shooting pain between my legs so bad that it destroyed my appetite, and embarrassment mingled with confusion. What, I wanted to know, were we celebrating? The clipping of my clitoris? That's what it had felt like. A deliberate violation. My mother was wolfing down her snack, thoroughly enjoying herself and the day. Watching her, I was thoroughly saddened. Did she know she had wronged me? Did Iago know he was evil? Did St. Joan know she was a saint?

"Here," I said none too gracefully, "you can have mine. I'm not hungry." There, I'd put a damper on her fun.

"But, darling, they're famous for cinnamon toast."

Mimicking her dulcet tones: "But, dahling, I don't give a cinnamon shit!" There. I'd really unsettled her Elizabeth Arden powder.

"Prudence! Lower your voice! You're too young to use that language."

The pot and the kettle. "Oh, but I *am* old enough for the gyno probe, I suppose. You certainly twist things according to your comfort."

"I just wanted you to be prepared," she said in a Billie Burke vague.

Articles, she read those, but not her daughter. It was her duty to know where I stood. "But you prepared me too soon! I'm not prepared to be prepared. I'm thirteen, for God's sake. I'm fat now and boys don't like me, and treats at Rumpelmayer's make me fatter. In four years I'll be ready, but not today!"

I was right on.

Four years later, prepared with the previously unused diaphragm my now uncaring mother had provided, I stopped in the kitchen to borrow two dollars from Selma to get to my lover.

"Thanks, luv, I'd do the same for you."

"Right on," she said as I closed the front door.

Traffic going downtown was impossible, and so was my cabdriver. He was a young hippie head type who kept trying to sell me a kilo of "the best grass off the market." I told him that I was very straight. He just laughed and looked at me in his mirror. After a while he said, "Nobody's straight, man. But nobody."

As I got out of the cab he insisted I take a card saying "Jesus Saves." On my way to sin, I took it.

Important men in New York are never on the first, second, or third floors. You really have to travel to get to them. Nate's offices were on the twenty-fourth floor—all of it. He headed a prosperous building and contracting firm. In the old days Lolly and I would frequently pass Spitz and Co. properties. She would station herself right beneath the sign and sing "My daddy built that building, my daddy built that building." Passing his buildings now, I get an urge to sing "My lover built that building, my lover built that building."

The Streaks 'n' Tips secretary wasn't as bad in person. She told me that I should go right in, and then, with a wink, that I was expected.

I couldn't resist a "Thanks, hon" as I passed her.

Nate was sitting at a huge desk, in a huge room, talking on the phone. He motioned me in, and it was the first time I noticed the pinky ring. I abhor jewelry on men. It should only be worn by gangsters and pimps and drag queens and Peter O'Toole in *Beckett.* One small accessory, an idiotic pinky ring, can throw a great deal off balance. Oh well, I thought, like that marvelous line that Joe E. Brown has at the end of *Some Like It Hot,* when he finds out that the woman he is smitten with is a man, "Nobody's perfect."

Nate was probably negotiating the war of the worlds over the phone. He was chain-smoking and perspiring heavily. I checked the room over, and it pleased me. A success room: good paintings, Bonnard, Dufy, a "blue period" Picasso, a powerful Dorthea Lang photograph of a blue-collar worker, and a canvas of Jamie

Wyeth's, who paints brilliantly but is relatively unknown. One thing a progressive, artsy-fartsy school teaches the precocious young is knowing good stuff from kitsch.

The family pictures on his desk brought me up short. I'd never actually seen Lolly's mother. She'd died of something frightful long before I came into view.

Discussing her with Lolly was absolutely *verboten,* and Nate and I hadn't gone into anything dark yet. It was a mystery around school as to what had actually caused her death, and I, being hyper-tuned in on hidden adult things, had a private suicide theory. An image of what she'd looked like had always stuck in the back of my mind—hanging from a rope with bright red, freshly applied lipstick on her mouth. When I was younger I didn't like spending the night at Lolly's. I was always afraid that we'd wake up dead in the morning. Children's fears are never quite outgrown, I don't think.

Standing there looking at the late Mrs. Spitz terrified me. She was a "sulky beauty," with masses of hair, "divoon" (my pixie friend again) cheekbones, and a nose that no surgeon could have touched. The whole pose looked more like a movie star still than merely "the Mrs." of Nate Spitz. It suddenly brought to mind Daphne du Maurier's *Rebecca,* and I . . .

"Jesus Christ, that raisin cunt. Tell her to take a douche! She's got no business being in a man's business if she can't stick to business! What? . . . No, she's not practical, she's an emotional mess, the bitch. Okay. Okay . . . Listen Fred, that contract has got to be signed by the twenty-eighth or we can't go with it . . . Well then, buy her out . . . money'll pay for a good sanitarium . . . Right, then you know where to go with it . . . Okay, Fred, good man . . . So long."

He sat back in his throne, grinning at me. The pinky ring, the picture, the last bit of his phone conversation, Lolly, they all seemed like red herrings. I had no idea who I was dealing with.

"Too much for you, Prude?"

"No! . . . What do you mean?"

"My language gets a little rough when I care a lot about something."

"Oh." I had thought he'd caught me staring at the picture. "Oh, no. It was high comedy."

"Now there you go, with your bastardized private-school phrases. It's not such a scream, I'll tell ya, when millions of dollars are mishandled." Nate always looked straight at me. "Never go into business, Puss," he said as his hand reached out.

I went toward it, clasped it, and with a nifty maneuver, got the ring off. He didn't even look surprised, just watchful. Men are not simple. "I don't like it."

"All right."

"Don't you want to know why?"

He had stood up over me, almost seeming to hold his breath. "Not at the moment."

He obviously was ready to have a little sexy-wexy. It happens still, when I get embarrassed, I use foolish terms for things like intercourse and menstruation. I felt huffy and giddy and rather damp below.

"Listen, Spitz, I came here on business—for the reading of my paper."

He smiled. "And the feeling in your loins."

He had a good smile, teeth in surprisingly fine shape . . . for his age, you know. It occurred to me that I kept making lists of his positive points. My position was of a professional debater who gets familiar with and cozies up to a subject only because he's stuck with it. Was this man who talked to Fred of douches the stuff that dreams are made of? I may be a New York sophisticate but I have a Disney soul. Had my theme song all along been "Someday Nate Spitz will come?"

He began doing lovely things to my body, new things he hadn't done the time before. I gave a high virginal sigh and went along with everything until we hit the floor. "Sorry, Spitz. I can't be passionate while my coccyx is breaking."

Abruptly he got up and walked away, and returned carrying a satin quilt and two matching satin pillows. I stifled an impulse to laugh at his tactics. Too many lunches at the Playboy Club. It was really rather touching. Men's fantasies about women are so remote. He lifted me high, and then set me down on our instant bed. He'd corrected something that had displeased me, which was nice.

I was feeling friendly as hell. "Listen, I'll take off my own clothes and you take off your own 'cause it's less clumsy and quicker."

He arched an eyebrow, and there was no smile. I waited for him to appreciate the fact that I'd just been appealing. No signs. There was too much of the wrong sort of silence. My imaginary tail stopped thumping. When he lit a cigarette he didn't close the lighter, he slammed it. I watched him smoke the entire "extra long" cigarette. I thought of my father and mother and of how they couldn't do anything with themselves, together. I thought of my diaphragm, which was probably in the wrong way. I thought of Lolly, whom I'd betrayed. I thought of Rebecca, who could have been my mother. I thought of someone who actually knew of, liked, and had purchased a Jamie Wyeth.

I tried to say the right thing. "I do not vant to be alone."

It worked. Although he tried to hide it, his mouth was twitching. "That's a lousy Garbo imitation."

I felt the order of things resume. "An impersonator, I'm not."

"No, you're very much Prudence Goodrich."

He was still acting like Mr. Sobersides. He reached for the pack.

"Please don't light another one."

"No?"

"No. What's going on?"

He sighed a giant cartoon sigh. Squatting in front of me, very smoothly, no knee creaks, he said without much expression, "I want to make love, for you."

I really creamed at that, "for you." It changed the whole meaning. "Thank you. You've just made my thingy throb."

"Clitoris."

"Okay, Henry Higgins, have it your way. Clitoris. But why does wanting to make you unhappy?"

"Because you're just young enough to be old."

I've always been gifted at understanding the obscure things people say, a real pro at interpreting subtext. Pinter's another one. Harold Pinter, Lolita, and I certainly would make music.

"What you mean is that you're scared because I'm not a chippy."

At that point we were lying down.

"Yes."

"Yes, but I'm not a woman either."

"You will be, Puss."

"You're invited."

"To what?"

"To my womanhood."

Somehow we'd moved to face each other, not yet touching, but in the pre-embrace position.

"Nate, your thingy just stood up."

"Penis, Prude."

"Ya. It just stood up."

"Say it."

"Penis."

"Say it again."

"Penis. Peeeeenis."

His breathing was getting a bit harder and his eyes were milky.

"Do you want to say other words, Puss?"

"Like what?"

"Well, like things you wouldn't say to your

mother. Words you've read about but haven't verbalized."

I was allowed. He had said I could. All the words that shocked and excited me. What an odd treat.

"I want to, but I have to turn away."

He put his arm around my back, drawing me into him. He took my finger and traced his lips with it. "I'd rather you didn't."

Actually, I felt quite at ease. Once permission has been given for anything, it's suddenly no big deal. "Okay. I'm ready, but I have to close my eyes." He laughed. "Take a deep breath," he said.

Two things occurred to me: that the little game was ludicrous, and that perhaps it was a format for arousing older men. So I went ahead, for his sake.

"Alrighty. Cock, prick, cunt, suck, twat, tit, pussy, sixty-nine, blow job, ummm . . . Oh, merkin and dildo. I've run out."

The older man I'd apparently just aroused had his eyes closed. His thingy felt very hard against my stomach. He stroked my bottom. "The last two won't do you much good, Puss."

"Nate, do you still want us to make love?"

For a moment I thought I'd put him to sleep. But then he did a grinding motion that reminded me of what all sixteen-year-old boys do on dance floors.

"Yes, but I also want us to fuck."

I recoiled. The word had such manual connotations: a construction worker doing it with his hard hat still on his head. "No! I don't want us to do that one bit!"

He still held me, but his body had lost its bull's anger. Eyes back in focus—I'd been worried there for a moment about glaucoma, not uncommon in the middle-aged male. With the palm of his hand, he smoothed my hair and then cleared his throat as if to banish his dirty old man voice. "You're a paradox, Prudence."

"Why? Because I get turned off by a manufactured turn-on?"

I'd expected him to bristle, but he didn't. He just kept palming my hair. "Not really. It's because you have such defined limits."

His hand was making my hair greasy. I took it and held it against my cheek. "Doesn't everybody?" I asked.

"No," he said dismally.

His body had collapsed. He was, then, very dear. Instinctively, I wanted to. I became the tender aggressor. Softly, and I hoped huskily, I said as a compromise, "Well, then, fuck 'em!"

I'd noticed for a long time that middle-aged men seemed to sense that I was playing in their camp. Perhaps though, suddenly, gray temples were the only possibility for me. I had no other frame of reference. I hadn't been a wallflower, I just hadn't cared. There had been no brother to rough me up, and then, at the blossom age, fix me up with his friends. No older "sis" to let me inherit what I didn't know. Of course, there was Lolly, who tried hard to compensate for my losses. She surely did try.

Two years ago Lolly was a self-educated siren. She was the sort of fifteen-year-old baby doll that statutory rape cases thrive upon. But she had no nymph problem. She was a very constant person, totally devoting herself to one boy for about two months, which at that age was longevity. She would moon and swoon, transforming every gangling Clearasil specimen into Rhett Butler. She had a way of making the average seem special. I always had a slight edge on her, though. I read all the time; I saw, I mean *really* saw and digested all that went on with the grownups, and I knew that most of what Lolly said was charming bullshit. And her repertoire was loaded with corny ruses.

Spring in New York is chillier than it should be and you can't leave that little sweater behind until early June. Well, Lolly would prance out in April in a sundress just to get some boy's skinny arm around her. Then she would sashay into a school dance smelling gloriously whorey, really scenting up the place. Someone would ask what *did* she have on, and she would say without a trace of tongue in cheek, "soap and water." I mean, Jesus! Yet everyone believed her. All the "try hard and fail" girls went home and hit the soap and water, never grasping why they still smelled like plain skin.

I never corrected her. I let her be superior to me. She needed to be . . . I was afraid of losing her.

We did most of our serious talking on the phone. Our frivolous chatting was done at "Jack's." The place was a somewhat greasy drugstore, not called "Jack's," but he was the man to see. He was the headwaiter, an ex-con with a multicolored tattoo on his arm saying "Inez, you're a hell of a lay." He wore a short-sleeved shirt that just managed to cover everything but "lay." Lolly captivated him, so he generously accepted me. Once I went in there alone. Jack wanted to buy me a Coke, but I refused. He shrugged and said, "That friend you got's the pretty one, but you got the smarts."

The two of us continued going in for a while, but I felt secretly smug after that. Jack had turned his favors. I was his ally, he knew where "I was at." Besides, he never said that I wasn't pretty really. It doesn't matter, I'm not. There's just too much going on with my face all the time. Only when I'm deadpan am I anything like conventionally pretty. Once the face is in motion, it's like a multiplication table. I know, because once I stood at the mirror talking with myself for about an hour, capturing every expression known to man. A person can't merely look at me and say, "Ahh, lovely." I get the subjective approach. People say, "Ya know who you look like????" . . . "Who?" I say, waiting for Venus de Milo. "You look *exactly* like my second cousin from Wrigley, Pennsylvania, who looks sad all the time 'cause her husband's on the front line."

To get back to how Lolly tried to make me a social success. She reminded me of a gracious lady cruise director, "Come on now, you two cerebral palsy victims, y'all get together. You two have a lot in common." Entire deals were negotiated in my honor. The most vivid one was the "Les Kessler Deal." We were high school freshmen at the time. Lolly was elected by a plurality vote to chair the social committee. It was such a coup because the girls who were usually voted in were juniors or seniors and had been "unofficially engaged" for at least a year. But again Lolly had captivated.

So being a social leader, she was privy to the *crème de la crème* of the neighboring boys' schools. During the first week of her reign she got pinned, and wore it smack on her right nipple (over clothes, no masochist she), which of course set a trend. All the "try hard and fail" girls, who probably gave out the goods for their pins, wore them in the identical spot that Lolly did and wondered why the pin drooped instead of sitting taut like Lolly's. As a very blue, very sharp Irish bar-owner friend of Nate's says, "It all adds up to a simple, fuckin' quality difference."

The fellow responsible for pinning Lolly was actually pretty decent—at least his credentials were. Carlton Janeway, Jr. He never quite liked me. I think I threatened him. I was the Best Friend of the girl he had the hots for and was trying to impress. He must have suspected that she told me All, which is rough on a peach-fuzz preppie. The All usually doesn't amount to much, and I think he knew that I knew it. He had an Englishman's attitude toward me: terribly polite, terribly cool, and would have terribly enjoyed giving me a stiff poke in the ass with an umbrella.

Lolly saw no wrong in Carlton. For all the wrong reasons. He was a straight-A junior at Collegiate, president of the Public Affairs Committee, president of the Social Committee, and president of his class, natch. With all that prestige, one didn't dare call him Carl. I did. He stung back, "What did you say, *Prude?*" I truly thank him for that. The nickname has a certain distinction which is becoming to me.

I must say, he did have brilliant hair. It was a cap of copper silk, worn faintly long, but still "kempt." Choirboy hair. He had a well-bred face, which means no sensuality. Thin lips, thin nose, thin eyes, etc. He was tall but hadn't filled out, making it difficult to judge his body possibilities. He was dressed exclusively by Brooks Brothers since infancy. His hands and feet were really nice, clean with square nails, also pedicured and manicured by Brooks Brothers. To sum up, Carlton looked like he just didn't go to the bathroom much.

His folks lived in one of the five best buildings on Park Avenue. It was, no doubt, the first best of the five, because they had old, old, old, old, old money. The "young folks" weren't allowed to sit on the living-room furniture, but the rug was better than most people's couches, so it worked out with no hard feelings. I somehow gracefully accept rules in other people's homes that I wouldn't tolerate in my own. Also, the treatment of other people's parents is a whole different language. You put your party manners on and try to impress the hell out of them. There's a universal story of a mother saying "Your friend Goodie is a delightful child," and the daughter seethes, knowing that Goodie is a monster in her own home.

And now the "Les Kessler Story" brought to you by . . . Actually, it was *The Eddie Duchin Story* that

I was glued to that fateful Saturday night. Since my social life was a stiff, I looked forward with zeal to Saturday Night at the Movies, a half a pound of William Greenburg cookies, and *real* coffee with a little brandy thrown in. I enjoyed my ritual tremendously, except during the holiday season. I was traditional when it came to that time of year, full of spiritual joys, with no one physical to give them to. Even at a tender fifteen I pictured myself thirty-five years later, basting a single turkey leg and ordering under another name gift-wrapped presents to be sent to me. Oh mama, I felt like Billie Holiday gettin' da blues real bad.

It was a December night, the folks were out, and I was hitting the brandy sans coffee. The *Duchin Story* is a real three-kleenex-boxer. Heavy, man, heavy. I was sobbing away during the commercial when my dear little Princess rang. It had to be Lolly.

"Prude?"

"No, I'm sorry. I think you must have the wrong number. This is Kim Novak. Prudence Goodrich is out tonight with Eddie Duchin." Lolly could always sense the times when I didn't feel very funny.

"Are you all right? Hey, are you crying?"

"No. I was just laughing until tears came at the Man from Glad."

"Oh. Well, tear yourself away from him and come over here."

"Where's here, Carlton's?"

"Of course, so get gussied up and come over. It's still early . . . and your Pair are out . . . and he wants you to."

"Who's He?"

"Carlton."

"Crap."

"No it isn't. He was the one who requested you. In fact, I'm beginning to wonder if he doesn't have a little crushie-poo on you."

Oh Jesus! She was using her whopper wiles.

"Nope. I don't want to. Besides, my father went bankrupt this morning and sold all my clothes. I can't. I don't want to. I think I'm pretty drunk." God, she could be persistent!

"All the better. Every party should have a drunk. Oh, come on, Prude—do it for me. I mean, what are friends for? Listen, just get yourself together, look gassy like I know you can, and be here. I love you and you know I'd do anything that you wanted me to . . . so . . . Okay?"

If I hadn't agreed, I knew that she'd be in a snit and would go off and have private lunches with Laverne Washington.

"The life of the party is on her way."

"Yea! I knew you would. Wear the orange."

"It's got a grotesque spot on it, but I'll just lie on my stomach the moment I walk in. You better tell Janeway to break out the Beluga."

"I will. Listen, Prude, I have to tell you. I'm bursting. Can you hear me?"

Lolly the conspirator.

"Yes. What is it?"

"Carlton fingered me tonight!"

"Oh yeah! I knew he would."

"But now I feel all funny—kind of . . . womanly, like I haven't in ages."

"That's nice. I'll be there in a little while. Bye."

"Wait, Prude? Listen, *please* don't tease your hair."

I arrived an hour later (had to see the end of the movie, which was not worth the cry) with balloon eyelids like a bad beautician's dream, looking almost totally dreadful. My shoes were nice.

Carlton was programed to open the door. It was only because of his breeding that he didn't make a nasty face.

"Hello, Prude. We're all glad you could make it."

"Why thank you kindly, Carl. I just hope I didn't miss most of the action."

He shot me one of his umbrella looks. "Not at all, not at all. In fact, we waited for you, Prude."

Boom! It dawned on me. There was a third "we" waiting for me in the living room. I was inclined to bolt, but one doesn't bolt on Park Avenue even if one is busted. It was a cruel trick, and determined to give the third "we" a very rough time, I entered the room.

"Prudie, Prudie." Lolly came gushing at me, all sloe-gin-fizzy and lipstick-toothed.

"We" stood up with outstretched hand, willing to make a go of it. "Hi, Prudence. I'm Les Kessler."

I decided to start in right away. "Hello, Lester. I don't shake hands since my accident. But when we get a little cozier you can call me Prudential."

He was not quite in Carlton's class. His face registered the put-down. Poor meatball. He'd probably been hijacked over there too. In fact, maybe he'd even been watching *The Eddie Duchin Story* and sobbing at the same time I was. His appearance wasn't a total loss. At least he looked like he ate a good thick sirloin once in a while.

The "you are what you eat" slogan is more evident in the male. Carlton looked like a cocktail olive; Nate looks like bluepoint oysters; Marvin, my father, is cherrystone clams; Barry Goldwater is fried clams at Howard Johnson's; and Richard Nixon is any sort of fowl . . . it can go on forever. Nate and I are avid players. We haggle a lot walking down the street saying "Asparagus." "No, no. All wrong. He's an obvious endive."

• • •

"Has anything hatched yet?"

"Huh? What?"

"I say, Prudential, has anything hatched yet in your nest?"

"You mean my hair?" He'd caught me off guard.

"Is that what you call it?"

He'd done it again. Mean. He'd decided to be a mean son of a bitch. I respected his choice. He gave me something to work with, to sharpen my wits on. Lolly and Carlton had somehow dematerialized to one of the chambers, leaving the new couple to couple. But once the first sparring was over, neither of us was sure if we should get bloody. He started walking around faking activity, picking up *objets d'art,* studying the paintings for too long. Every time he'd turn his back, I'd try to flatten down my hair. He began to get desperate, having looked at everything in the entire room. Then he fingered the drapes for a time and stooped to feel the carpet. Finally inventory was over. He took out a pack of Benson and Hedges and sat down near me.

"Cigarette?"

"Not that kind. My tongue gets caught in the filter."

"You're right. People with plump tongues should stay clear of these."

Apparently he'd caught a second wind, ready to start up again. I felt a bit wilted. I wanted a grownup. Of course, at that time I wasn't ready yet for the kind of man I needed, but I had a firm conviction that the Les Kesslers and all my other peers were from hunger, and that "my person" would relieve me of them forever.

"Anything your tongue can do, mine can do better. Gimme a cigarette."

He really blew the single-handed match light, which I roared about, saving him no embarrassment. He lit another match and held it out to me. Just as I started sucking for it, he blew it out.

"Ya know, Kessler, you're a b–"

"Only because you're a bitch."

"Ah, but you didn't let me finish, Kessler. I wasn't about to call you a bastard, that would be too much of a compliment. I mean I know people who are very much in love who say 'you bitch,' 'you bastard,' and then they go to bed. No, I was going to say that you're a bore. You are. You're really boring."

That got to him. He reached out and yanked my hair, which certainly got a rise out of me. I reached out and boxed his ear, an action straight from Dickens.

"Shit. That hurt! What was that?"

"It's called a boxed ear, Kessler."

He held his ear with both hands. His eyes were watering slightly. "Why did you do that?"

"Because along with the other B's, you're a baby."

The situation was beyond salvaging, so I decided to go home. I stood up, holding out my hand. "Good-bye, Kessler. Fuck you very much for the nice time."

I still offered my hand, giving him one last chance to get back at me. Had he been with it, he would have known judo, would have taken my hand and thrown me. Instead, he just sat there rubbing his ear, muttering something about sticking to Macdonald's hamburgers.

I was getting my coat from the hall closet when Carlton appeared, smelling like Lolly and semen and Le Courvoisier brandy. I suppose he'd heard his buddy's cry, and leaving a languishing Lolly, had come out to be a good host. Having had his way with my best friend, he assumed a brotherly air toward me.

"Hey, Prudie, what's this?"

"This, Carlie, is called grabbing my coat and splitting. Tell Lolly to call me tomorrow for the weather report."

He was playing it to the hilt, but for the first time I felt something genuine coming through. He was really looking at me.

"What's happening?"

"It happened already. I've gotta go."

He took my hand, no longer a cocktail olive. No, he'd graduated to one of those jumbo black pitted kind. "Why don't you stay for a little bit longer and have something to eat. Lol's going to make scrambled eggs and we have smoked salmon and cream cheese and stuff. I'll put you in a cab later."

I fought for the familiar protection. "Well, that sounds pretty good. Which dining room are you serving it in?"

His face changed. The umbrella look was back. "I guess you're not very hungry."

"Nope. Oh, say, I meant to tell you. *Five Finger Exercise* is on television next week. Good movie. You'll like it."

In the elevator going down, the night man had to lend me his handkerchief.

There is a type of person who, if asked whether they like Scarlatti, will say "Which one?" This type of person is a phony. True, there are two Scarlattis, but so what? Intellect is often used as a lid, covering a pot, preventing anything from possibly boiling over. So what's wrong with boiling over? So you wipe it up. Nate Spitz is a great wiper-upper. He has to be. He's the one who started taking off my lids.

Nate is bright enough to relax with himself. He can recognize a conversation that could get phony, and sidestep it.

"Nate, do you like Scarlatti?"

"Yes, Puss, I certainly do . . . But only with white clam sauce."

Oh yes, I started to be very much in like with Nate Spitz.

We were together one afternoon (I had cut school, he had cut the office) walking along 57th Street, playing the food game, when Mrs. Roger Lattimer saw us. BaBa Lattimer's mother. I had dropped BaBa about two months before because she had campaigned against a girl who was very together and extremely well suited for a certain office. The girl just happened to be black. I never had quite understood what BaBa was doing at our school anyway. In the first grade, during the Eisenhower-Stevenson election, she had come to school sporting an oversized jewel-encrusted "I Like Ike" button. I should have known then. Mrs. Lattimer's political, sexual, and religious demeanors were block-printed on her face: reactionary, frigid, and confession box.

We were arm-in-arm crossing the street. She was coming out the side entrance of Tiffany's. She did a take that caused other people on the street to glance at us. She would have been pleased to have been holding a camera. I was prepared to cut her dead, but not Nate. Behaving as though he were in a small town, he tipped his hat and said, "How-do, Mrs. Lattimer. How's every little thing?" She turned and marched back into Tiffany's. Nate made me walk on—well, he walked on. I was jumping up and down like a mad thing, whimpering and moaning.

"Ohhhh, Naaaaate. Ohhhh."

"Having trouble, Puss? Do you have to go that badly?"

I wondered if anything shook him. "Come on. Don't kid about it! She *saw* us! Maybe you're just in shock."

He put my arm through his. "It takes a lot more than that to shock me. So what if she saw us?"

"But . . . she really *saw* us!"

"So did everyone else on the street."

"But they don't *know* us."

"Neither does she."

I guess he noted that I wasn't holding up very well. "Hey! Taxi!" He held the door for me.

"What did you do this for?" I asked, feeling as though I were being smuggled.

Nate slid in beside me. "I wanted to neck."

"No. Come *on!* Don't you even care?"

He lit me a cigarette. "Not that I'm aware of. What's to care?"

I pursued it. "That she'll tell."

"No, she won't," he said with finality.

"She told Tiffany's."

I destroyed him with that one. He laughed for three blocks, mopping up his eyes at the red light.

"It's not funny. Why did she go back in there then?"

"Probably to have a good pee and let it all out."

"She'll tell. I bet she made a phone call in there."

He lit me another cigarette. "I doubt it. Not one phone works in that store. They have two phones and both are out of service."

"Oh." I sat back for a second, waiting to return to normal.

"Hey, what were you doing in Tiffany's?"

He blew a series of once-in-a-lifetime smoke rings. "That's for me to know and you to find out."

"When's that?"

"When you stop being afraid of some raisin cunt who will never tell a soul. *And* when you start being unafraid of what we're doing."

He turned abruptly away, looking out his window. A fraught moment was on us. I looked out my side window, waiting until it passed. Suddenly he ducked, landing with his head in my lap. "Quick, quick, hide me!" His head lurched under my coat and dress.

"Hey, what the hell are you doing. A grown man! What's up?"

Still under my dress, he gave a muffled but accurate imitation of my whiny voice. "The butcher. My butcher! He just saw us! He'll tell!"

God, what a darling man I had under my dress. "But, Nate, we're in a moving taxi."

"He has quick eyes."

"Well, I think it's safe to come out now. We passed him blocks ago."

"But the cleaner. The cleaner might just be walking down this block."

We were both giggling. Even the cabdriver was having a good *yuk*. By doing his damndest, Nate had made me see the absurdity of worrying about other people's thoughts. He would have been a fine teacher. Show and Tell; it's the only way to catch on.

"Hello in there. You can come out now."

Emerging, his well-groomed hair in spikes, he offered one last ridicule. "Ohhh, the cabdriver! He saw us!"

I put my arms around his neck, smoothing his hair, giving him soft little kisses. "You know what? You are my best friend."

He took my face and gave me a hard, long "starting of passion" kiss. After it, he still held my face. "Now, does a best friend do that?"

"No."

"Who does?"

It was hard for me, but this was not a Les Kessler. "My man does," I said.

Nate was right, as it turned out. Mrs. Robert Lattimer might have told the Pope to tell God about it, but she didn't tell anyone that we knew.

• • •

Lolly continued not to acknowledge me. I discussed her with Nate at first, but the deeper our involvement became, the farther away she got.

She held out with a vengeance. I got the silent-freeze treatment. But I held out too, and every time I'd see her I'd smile and say "Hi." She never turned anyone else against me though, which was thoughtful, because no matter how bright and how liberal, girls of seventeen in an all-girls high school can be lethal.

For a while I thought that I could bring the old Lolly back, but the while was over and I realized that she was through with me. She was being loyal to her father, and that was all. Montague/Capulet, Goodrich/Spitz.

She'd formed other close friendships. I hadn't. Not that I went around with a scarlet letter on my forehead. I still had friends, but very casual ones. After all, I was a woman of affairs, with little time for pillow fights and making fudge.

When I didn't sit alone in the lectures, I sat with Naomi Jenks. She was a sculpture major who only sculpted busts of herself. I suppose she was working things out. She was always very calm. Nate says those are the kind who are sexually pagan, the very tranquil ones.

Much later, after we'd started saving seats for each other in all the lectures, Naomi told me her story. Apparently she'd had three abortions, at ages fourteen, fifteen, and sixteen, all caused by the same guy. Calm, nothing! It was a wonder that she could walk around.

She asked me to come into the art studio one morning to see a figure she'd just finished. Again it looked exactly like her. But it wasn't only a bust, she'd sculpted her whole body, standing up, with arms closed around a distended belly.

I smiled, feeling like a therapist after a breakthrough. "Wow, Naomi, it's beautiful. It should be in a gallery."

She smiled back. "Right now that kind of thing doesn't matter. See, I've been going through some rough changes and I can't afford to get help. I'm on scholarship here as it is. But see, when I finally spilled out to you, I was free to make this. That's what matters."

I told Nate about it. The next day a gift arrived for me. A bunch of Band-Aids in a fourteen-karat-gold case.

It was February. February is not a month. It is a long bad mood.

I'd gotten home late one afternoon after dragging through my three hours of volunteer work at Columbia-Presbyterian Hospital. My assignment there was in a male ward. It was far different from the kind where the GI's sit up in bed, whistling and making kiss sounds and wanting to date you after they recover, and the one you fall for is John Garfield. No way. These beds were filled with New York's worst. These were the self-destructive ones. These were the now helpless victims of the city. It could have easily been mistaken for a mental ward, it was that bad. When I got home, I would take baths all night and not touch my dinner.

That afternoon had been only slightly worse than the others, but it had really gotten to me. I walked straight to my room, shut the door, and began to cry. At first it was the dry kind, with no sound. Then I got going and worked up to hysteria. When I decided that I'd had enough, I couldn't stop. My period wasn't due, I wasn't pregnant, nobody had died . . . I gave up. Sitting on the edge of the bed with my winter coat still buttoned, I sobbed and sobbed.

"Prude? Can I come in?"

Marvin was at my door. (My mother was behind *her* door.) Marvin, my father, was a writer. He worked at home, trying his best not to be disturbed. He'd gone away to write his last book, though, which had been a best seller.

"Prude?"

"What?"

"Do you want me to come in?"

I nodded the affirmative, still convulsed with emotion.

"What?"

"Yes, Daddy."

As soon as I saw him, it made me start up full force again. He came over and started getting me out of the coat; it was like manipulating a rag doll. Once it was off, he sat down and took me in his arms, letting me drool and sputter all over his cashmere sweater. He just held me, not saying anything. The attack began to subside.

"Oh, Daddy, I disturbed your work."

"Don't be so silly."

He wiped my nose with his hanky.

"Will this one be another best seller, do you think?"

He chuckled. "For that, I'll have to go away again. Now, do you know what's behind all this carrying on?"

"I know . . . and I don't know."

"Have you tried to dope it out?"

"Well, I know the major trauma but not why I'm still screaming from it."

He propped me up with some pillows and brought the desk chair over for himself. "Okay. What did you do today?"

"I got up."

"And then what?"

"Went to school."

"And then?"

"Well . . . I had lunch."

"Who did you have it with?"

"With . . . Laverne . . ."

Lunch. That must have been part of it. I was to have had lunch with Nate, but some business thing had come up and he'd canceled me. I thought I'd been able to shrug it off. What a bitch the psyche is.

Daddy and I looked at each other. Jesus, did he know how to read me. He knew I'd hit on something and had gotten over the hump. But not being an obvious man, he kept on. "Then what, baby?"

"Well, I had to go to Columbia-Presbyterian."

"Did anything upset you there?"

"Absolutely."

"What happened?"

"Well, it's always awful and I hate it. Hate it! But today they made me turn over this scabby old man from his back to his stomach. And the volunteers aren't really supposed to do that kind of messy thing, but if you complain, they tell the school, and your mark goes down."

Marvin cracked a knuckle for emphasis. "That's unreasonable. But get back to the scaggy old man."

He was contributing, which meant that I'd seduced his lively writer's imagination. Marvin was scornful of the mundane. That someone missed their bus or that the soup was cold left him nowhere. The somewhat bizarre interactions in life excited him enormously.

"Scabby not scaggy. Anyway, I went over to the old fart and started to turn the sheets back so I could get a grip on him. His eyes were closed and there was caked yellow spittle all down his chin. He was Gandhi-thin, so I thought there'd be no problem flipping him over. I just hoped he wouldn't wake up and ask for his daughter, or his mangy old dog, or his opium."

Marvin laughed at my descriptive padding.

I chastised him. "Wait, it's not funny."

He pulled the corners of his mouth down with his fingers. "Of course it's not. Go on."

I'd stopped with the self-pity and was devoted to the telling of a good story. "So then . . . just as I'd put my hands gently on his shoulders, trying to avoid the oozing bedsores, and just as I was about to say a comforting 'upsy-daisy,' he cackled and mumbled something. I bent my head, trying to pick up on it. That was my mistake, not to ignore him. With his eyes still closed, he grabbed my hand in the Geriatric Grip, and repeated it: 'Didn't say may I.' Okay, so with my hand in his bony vise I tried to be sunny and breezy like the R.N.s should be but aren't. 'You're pretty sharp for an old codger. All right, may I? So *then*—Oh, Daddy! He grabbed my hand and rubbed it all over his parts, saying 'You may, you may, you may.' He wouldn't let go! He should be brought up on charges, making me give him a feel like that!"

My father looked faintly amused, but his voice was serious baritone. "And then what did you do?"

"I ran to the bathroom, soaked my hand in boiling water to sterilize it, and then stuck my finger down my throat to throw up lunch."

My father registered mirth. "An excellent denouement! That's quite an episode, quite a little hair-raiser."

I felt tired. Emotions wear you out. "You can go back to work now, Daddy."

He stood up into a stretch. "Nah, I'm through for today. Can't be creative in February. Anyway, it's almost dinnertime, and yes, you may be excused from it. Why don't you take one of your many baths and then hop under the covers for a while?"

His attention was already out of the room. "To take the chill off," I said to myself.

He came over, gave me a hug, and then opened the door.

"Daddy?"

"What?"

"I love you much."

He nodded. "Returned in full."

Exit.

Later, in bed, it grabbed me. I'd been making some psyched-up connection between Nate and that dirty old man.

I stopped myself. The old man was the old man. Nate was Nate and Daddy was Daddy. And that was that.

Every relationship arrives at a point where it either leaps ahead or it peters out. "The road not taken" bit makes all the difference. Petering is hardly ever mutual. One party instigates it, the other is forced to follow suit.

I do believe that Nate and I were unique from the beginning. I was seven, he was thirty-five. He took Lolly and me for a pony ride at the zoo. Our first meeting. He tells me, romantically if not accurately, that he refused to allow the pony's owner to lift me into the saddle.

"Nate, I was seven years old, for God's sake!"

"Youth always gives me a hard-on, Puss."

"You are profane!"

"No. I'm practical."

"You mean you knew then that I'd grow up to be me?"

"I knew that I'd wait around to find out."

"You were insane!"

"No. I was hopeful."

During March there wasn't a day that Nate and I didn't communicate. When he had wall-to-wall appointments, he would send flowers or a telegram. Once I got a dolly-gram, which is a small stuffed toy wearing the message in its paws, or mouth, or some cutesy thing. I resented it.

"You know that thing you sent me yesterday?"

"What?"

"That dummy dolly thing."

"Oh, right. Western Union with a flair. Didn't you like it?"

"*No*. As a matter of fact, it was unnecessarily patronizing. I am quite beyond toys."

We were at a restaurant, which we usually didn't do because of my homework. We finished the meal in silence. The waiter came with dessert menus.

Nate addressed me formally. He never did that.

"Dessert, Prudence? Or does that fall under the childish category?"

"No, thank you. I'm full."

I didn't want what was happening. I had deliberately provoked friction, which is a parent/child trend. It really turned Nate sour.

He excused himself and went off to the men's room and I sat there for what seemed like a very long time, with a new kind of pain. I'd hurt someone but it was my pain. Maybe he'd gone out the back exit. Maybe he was fed up with being "the older man." I guess I loved him. He was *not* my father.

Sometimes, in a really piss-elegant restaurant, you can get away with anything. I read the dessert menu. The prices were high enough to be eccentric. When I thought the coast was clear, I slid across the table into his seat and wrote on the tablecloth with my eye pencil:

Humbert, come home!
Lolita wants her dessert.
She also wants you.

I saw Nate and hopped back to my place before he saw me. Cross those fingers and toes, girl! My heart was transplanting itself. I held my breath. At first I thought perhaps he'd taken care of the check and wasn't going to sit down. I said a little something to

God and Nate sat down. He seemed to be looking for the waiter to give us our check. He hadn't glanced down and he didn't even have his glasses on. Shit. I should have written it larger. Shit. The waiter had seen him. Shit. God? Oh, please tell Nate Spitz to put his glasses on before the waiter at the French restaurant on —I think it's 54th Street and Lexington—gets to our table. Nate took out his glasses. Shit. He was going to wipe them. *No!* God, there's no time for polishing. Nate put his glasses directly on.

"Nate?"

"Um?" He wouldn't look at me.

"Nate, I think the check is on the tablecloth in front of you."

He looked down and saw the message. His mouth twitched. It was going to be all right. God? Any time you need a favor. . . .

In keeping with the precision of the whole evening, the waiter then advanced toward us.

"The lady has changed her mind—women always do. Bring the pastry tray for her. Just coffee for me."

Nate didn't say anything else, but his hand rested, very lightly, on my knee.

He walked me home, holding my fingers, bringing them to his lips every so often. We were going to keep a lookout for a taxi, but the air felt too good and we were both mellow as hell. We didn't talk much, just breathed a lot. He would stop, whimsically, in the middle of the sidewalk, drawing me inside his coat, kissing and touching.

"Watch that. We'll be arrested."

"For what?"

"For enjoying ourselves."

We reached my block. It had been an important walk. Nate hesitated slightly by feeling his pocket. Men always feel their pockets. It's nerves.

"Aren't you going to walk me to my door?"

"Yes, of course I am."

I took his arm. "Well . . ."

"First I want you to listen to something, Puss, not only hear, but really listen."

"Shoot."

He lit a cigarette. I'd noticed that whenever he wasn't sure of how I was going to react to something, he gave me a little cancer. "Only when you're truly beyond having toys and such are you able to take joy in them, and to value that joy."

I had one of those flash images of the two of us bedding down with huge stuffed animals, and dinghy cars, and yo-yos.

"Why are you smiling? Do you think what I said is amusing?"

"Not at all. It was pretty serious. A double entendre, wasn't it? Or was it a metaphor?"

He smiled, what they call ruefully. "A bit of both, Puss."

I felt I needed to break his mood. He was getting awfully rueful. It was European and wearily sexy but it wasn't Nate.

"Ya know, Spitz, you're not bluepoint oysters at all."

"No? After careful consideration, I thought we'd decided that I couldn't be anything else?"

I began to circle around him, observing, checking him up and down. Jesus, I loved the way he looked. Most of the time. On the days that he had a big deal to consummate, he would get himself up like the manager in chief of the Nunn Bush shoe stores. All spit, polish, tie tacks, and pinky rings. When he slipped and looked that way, I wondered what I was doing with him. No longer Nate but Flash or Lefty. But when he did a full hour of exercises and took his Librium, he was "just my Bill." Well toned, yet relaxed and rumply. He would wear gray flannel slacks, a navy turtleneck, and a full head of well-barbered more pepper than salt hair. He would take a thirsty last drag on his Chesterfield cigarette, letting the smoke rampage through his nostrils. He would put aside the Sunday *Times* Real Estate section. He would need a shave. He would reach for me. Never handsome. Better. His face looked lived in. The lights were on in his eyes.

He stopped my motion. "You're making me dizzy. Let's hear the verdict. What am I?"

Just then a standard poodle that we hadn't seen started to lift a dignified leg on Nate, who jumped back with a roar. The owner, an aging blonde, jerked the dog's leash, saying something boring like "Bad dog! Almost did on the nice man." The two of them walked on.

I gave Nate lots of kisses, smoothing his feathers. "That's probably how an old prostitute does business."

There, I'd made him laugh. I was good for him most of the time. I was almost sure I was.

"You still haven't told me what I am, Puss."

"Well, you almost were a hydrant, yuk, yuk. Okay. I'll tell you, but let's walk down."

We skipped instead, because he'd forgotten to do his workout that morning.

"You are not an appetizer. You are a mother of a meal, with so many courses . . . that it takes forever to finish."

We were at the door. I fished for my keys. I couldn't remember ever having been so aware of him as I was that night.

"Whew! So many head games, Nate."

"Maybe. But useful ones."

He put my key in the lock, goosing me at the same time. Squealy and squawky, I whipped around and flung myself on him like a mad thing unfurled. "Oh, honey, ohhh, hoooneee." I ruffled and bit and chewed and caressed. I was giving a marvelous imitation (I should hope to tell you) of a couple we'd watched waiting in a movie line the previous week. The girl had been beside herself with lust; the man, beside himself with embarrassment. He'd stood immobile, his Adam's apple doing push-ups. Nate had thanked me for being me.

So as I was progressing with my charade and had involved myself in blowing on his chest hairs, I heard him say very softly, "Whoa, Prude."

The original male voice came from behind me. "I believe I've seen this young man before." The father had spoken.

An ideal tableau for a confession magazine's cover story: "Caught Between Her Two Men—Devil or Angel?"

After several beats of well-kept silence, we all behaved diplomatically. At that late hour almost anything said would be held against us the next day. I surprised myself by not breaking into paroxysms of nervous titters, but my entire womanhood seemed to be at stake. I thought of Madame Bovary and posed accordingly.

Nate emerged from a bemused retirement, to shake my father's hand, and to say that yes, they'd briefly met at one P.T.A. or another.

Marvin said wryly, "They all look the same," and they both chuckled a shade too heartily and much too long. I felt like breaking out the port. Marvin offered a nightcap, which was a bit schmoozy of him but altogether decent. Nate declined with an Old World hand gesture implying that he didn't touch spirits, which must have put my father on the defensive, because he didn't volunteer a "some other time." I was relieved to see that at that point Nate revved up some charm, saying, "No, thanks, really. I was just going and your daughter was just staying."

They shook parting hands. It was all very ceremonial. "Goodnight, all," my father said wisely, padding down the hall then and leaving me to my beloved.

Cast in his new role as the suitor, Nate circled my waist with his arm, keeping a gentle distance between us. "When's your next date with the Doc, Puss?"

"Day after tomorrow, two to two-fifty."

He was poker-faced. "If I were you, I'd discuss your tablemania."

"My what?"

"Writing on tablecloths. That's serious stuff." He winked, and was gone.

The door to my room was open. Something was very much up, because I always kept it closed to insure the privacy of my gifts from Nate. My father was sitting at my desk, all hunched over, with his back toward me. I knocked to announce my entrance; having no words seemed the best way to begin. Perry Mason always tells his clients who might be found guilty to shut up rather than implicate themselves.

My prosecutor turned around, looking just like a distraught parent. "Take a seat, my lady of the night," he said, maintaining his style.

"I'd rather take it standing up, sir," I said, maintaining mine.

We both waited, like two actors who had gone dry in their lines. Prompter, prompter! It would have been easier if we'd been able to be primitive: ("I'll get the strap, girl . . .").

"How long has this been brewing, baby?"

He obviously wasn't going to whup me. Why was he so criminally understanding? It made things much harder. To be forgiven is very hard to take. "You mean with Nate?" I asked. Did I see him flinch at the sound of a name not his own?

"With Lolly's father, yes."

I sat down for his comfort. "Well, to be thorough with my answer, since I was about seven. But we waited for me to grow up before doing anything. It really took off this past fall."

Marvin kept looking at his bedroom slippers—how vulnerable I'd made him. I offered him one of my "extra longer Nate cigarettes," wishing I could offer him more of myself to make up for what I'd done.

"You haven't *done* anything," he said, latching onto the vibe. "It's just that I have to get familiar with my reactions."

I had school the next day. "I wish this had happened on a Friday night."

My father got up with a spiritual arthritis. "I wish it hadn't happened," he said bluntly. And then, "But since it has, I'm glad that he's got a decent handshake."

In bed, I sang softly:

"And she wheeled her wheelbarrow
Through streets broad and narrow
Crying Na-ate and Daddy, alive, alive O . . ."

The next morning I did not oversleep. I overlaid. I was fully awake, knew I'd be late, but I liked the way my mind was working while my body was relaxing. I do my very best thinking on the toilet, with lying down a close second. At forty bucks an hour, lying down, you learn to think v-e-r-y well. Here's why I think doctors never say much: they fall asleep sitting up after they've trained you to babble away lying down.

I had finally left the bed, and stood, naked, wondering what to do first. Enter Mother. Not typical. She usually slept it off until every afternoon. "It" wasn't alcohol. "It" was severe depression. She was all dressed and even had make-up on. Too much of it.

"You're late. You overslept. What are you doing?"

That staccato phrasing should have been a warning to me. Self-involved as I was, I still ought to have known.

"What I'm doing, Mother, is not talking to you right now. I wish you wouldn't do this."

She looked strange. I didn't notice then but I remembered afterward.

"Do what?"

"Barge in here."

"Why? Because you don't have any clothes on?"

"Yes, partly."

"Masturbation is natural, dear."

She was just standing there saying "on the brink" things, and all I could be was annoyed.

"Mother, I'm trying to get dressed!"

"I'm your mother."

"Jesus! What does that mean?"

"Your body came out of *me*. Then it was naked. I'm your mother. You'd better hurry, dear."

"Then *let me!*"

"I'm helpful—trying to be."

For a second I must have felt a twinge. On my way to the closet, I kissed her rouged cheek. "I know you are. Could I have some coffee maybe?"

She'd turned and walked out, never answering. But she'd somehow gotten a cup together and stood by me as I drank it. "Is it good?"

"Ya. It's instant coffee."

"Is it strong?"

"Ya."

"Hot? Is it hot, dear?"

How awful for her. She'd been unable to stop.

"Um."

"I don't see any steam."

"Well . . ."

"It wasn't hot. It wasn't good, was it?"

"Mother, it's only a fucking cup of coffee! Holy Jesus!"

She sat down. I got up.

"Listen, don't worry about it. I'm off."

"You're always off," she said with more whine than wasp.

But it was a detainer and I had to give it time. "I manage to keep myself busy, Mother. Would you want an idle, shiftless daughter?"

She answered, falling on top of my words as though she'd been lying in wait—a scrapper with fists up before the first blow, "No, just a less secretive one. One who talks to her mother instead of banishing her. I just want a friend." I was about to be moved when she spoiled it. "I want to meet your boyfriend. I'm good with boyfriends."

My familiar contempt slid back in place. "I abhor that word! It's cheesy."

She wouldn't let go. "But you do have one. Busy people have things, boyfriends. I used to." She was rapidly losing ground.

I gave her another kiss on that poor painted cheek. "Good-bye, friend," I said.

She let go. "Good-bye, dear. I'm sorry as hell about the coffee."

I left her.

I went into analysis when I was sixteen. I should have gone when I was six when the term "problem child" arose frequently. I'd been a fanciful child. The people around me hadn't the know-how to cope with my world. At that age a child just doesn't say, "Hey, do you know of a good shrink?" So I pretended to straighten out until I was sixteen, when Marvin could afford to pick up the tab. I'd lived through eight unhealthy years, packing down all the reasons for all the rage.

My mother had, up until the black-patch caper, been a high-fashion model. She met my father through an interview. He, a young columnist on the *Herald Tribune,* had been assigned to write a piece on the professional "beautiful, empty" people. How they lived their lives, what they ate, who they loved, etc. She had been on his list of subjects. At that last minute another of the models had dropped out to have a nervous breakdown, so my mother got an extra-long session. I guess he became infatuated when he discovered that her sentences had subjects, predicates, and verbs. She kept throwing the interview off by asking about him, and the day after they'd covered the necessary format, he phoned her, saying that he needed more material. They were together all that day. His final question was the clincher.

"Are you in love at the moment?"

She must have been very beautiful, very unattainable.

"Yes, I am."

"May I ask who with?"

"You may."

"Who?"

"You."

Just recently Daddy told me that if any other woman had fed him that line he would have rolled her once in the hay and that would have been that. But he said that she'd really seemed to mean it, and she'd looked kind of frail and tubercular, and he'd felt compelled to take care of her until she was stronger.

What a crock! He *married* the lady. Oh, I think what he says is half true. The other half was that he fell madly in love with her.

"Orthodox" is not part of my vocabulary. Everything that touched me was tinged with a bit of madness. Nothing concrete, nothing I could point to, but always hovering.

My parents adhered to the Mr. and Mrs. America patterns, I'll vouch for that. We had Thanksgiving and Christmas and birthday parties. But Thanksgiving dinner meant lobster or quail; the gifts under the Christmas tree were never wrapped; at my birthday parties my mother booked fashion shows instead of magicians. My mother kept losing her looks. My father kept hauling out old albums of her photographs to remind her of her beauty. Like tutor and invalid pupil he would say, "Look here, there's you at the Chanel show in '48." She would say slowly, "Oh, yes . . . I see."

The more my father wrote, the more my mother did nothing.

We would eat dinner shockingly late according to me. I mean, the school lunches should have been investigated by Nader's Raiders. I never touched them, so by three P.M. I was hungry. I was swamped with homework, which I had to do on an empty stomach. My mother never kept the usual crap around (a habit from her emaciated modeling days). It was dinner or nothing. The kids from normal homes would have supper at six-thirty and *then* do the bulk of their homework. In my family, by the time we put down our napkins it was ten—on a good night.

It all had a manic logic. Inspiration came to my father late in the afternoon. Awareness came to my mother at about the same time. Both began their day in the early evening.

Dinner conversation was stimulating. Lots of silence. Background instrumentals on the cutlery. Selma would serve when she felt like it—when she didn't, we'd walk into the dining room, a buffet would be laid out on the sideboard, and we wouldn't see her until the next night.

None of us displayed an appetite at the table. We were all "drawer" eaters: Marvin kept a miniature fridge in his den, stocked with Sara Lee Banana Cake and Schweppe's Bitter Lemon; my mother stashed a box of bone-dry Grapenuts in with her sacheted lingerie; and my specialty was Schrafft's butter crunch that I'd buy in bulk blocks, breaking it off until my index finger got red and sore.

But during the meal we all fasted. My mother would suck every piece of ice from her water glass. My father would drag on his cigarette between bites.

"Did you write today, Marvin?"

"Yes."

"Oh. Good."

"What about you? Did you do your nothing today?"

"Yes."

The tension, along with my hollow stomach, usually made me feel queasy. I would say, "I gotta be excused."

Daddy would agree and say, "I'll be in later."

He would keep his word more often than not, coming into my room to listen to my side of life. He would give me fifteen minutes. I used to time it. He was loving, but always once removed. When he didn't come in, I knew he'd gone out for the night.

Money kept our home together. It made everyone shut up. I suppose my father bought mistresses; mother bought cosmetics; I bought an analyst.

We had a scare once, back in the early fifties, when my father's name was mentioned during the blacklistings. He made his entire living as a free-lance author. Being that he was his own man, belonging to no one, made him an immediate suspect. He also voted a straight Democratic ticket and wore his hair long. I remember a variety of men coming to our house to snoop around. It was handled tastefully, of course, no Gestapo tactics. They would pose as magazine or newspaper scouts trying to lure Daddy into writing subversive articles that would incriminate him. They offered exorbitant fees. He always told them to stick it.

There was a key witness to the case, however. Someone who saw to it that he was let completely off the hook. That person was . . . dum da dum dum . . . my mother. At school, whenever I told the story, I would be the center of attention. I told it once too often.

I approached this girl at recess. She had just transferred from another school into our grade. Rumor had it that she was a scholarship case. She wrote with pencils that had no erasers. That's all I'd chosen to notice about her. Oh, her name. Greta Salakchi. I'd looked it up on the attendance list. To Lolly: "Singer sewing machine clothes and she doesn't smile . . . when you're new, you should smile."

Nefertiti to handmaiden: "Her name's too hard to pronounce."

Lolly seemed to leave invisible slogans in the air: "To notice is human. To ignore is divine."

Greta was sitting alone in the math room eating a five-cent candy bar. She was enjoying it in the quietest, fullest way I'd ever seen anything be eaten. She made me let her finish it before I could speak. I was adept at telling my story; it was an old standard. She crumpled up the wrapper, aiming for the wastebasket. In.

"Hi, Greta, wanna hear a story that's truer than nonfiction?"

She made me nervous. She wasn't a regular girl.

"Why not?" then she scraped her hair back tight, holding it with her hands. "First, let's have a name for you."

Jesus! She was all but killing my performance.

"Oh . . . Hi! I'm sorry! . . . I'm Prudence . . ."

Her legs weren't shaved well.

"Then what?" she asked.

I wished I hadn't started. "Then what what?"

"Your surname—what is it?"

"Goodrich."

Did she smile? Had I given something away?

"Let's have it, Prudence. I'll listen."

I had been inquisitioned. Funny now, but weak like flannel then. At a castanet clip, I was halfway through when she did one of those quirks only becoming to outcasts. She spit. Real saliva that went slashing across my shoe. I would have laughed "scoffingly" had I known her intent in advance. But my honest surprise allowed her the top card. Card shark.

"That's chicken shit!" She looked choleric as hell. "I happen to have a father who *is* blacklisted! Not *almost!* He probably won't ever be able to get a decent job again."

Then, not for the ears of babes, "So up your giggy with a meat hook, Prudence Goodrich!"

I'd never heard the term "giggy" before but I knew immediately what and where it was. For all of my attempt at the casting away of breeding, I was indignant. I didn't want to have a giggy.

Lolly had thoughts about it. Sitting Zen fashion on her canopy bed in pure white dancer tights, with clean white breath: "She was trying to make a pass at you, Prude."

(Lolly did lots of undercover reading.)

"You mean she's dykey?" (So did I.)

We got up simultaneously to close the door to her room. We should have formed a sister act with fans or something, our timing was perfect. With Lolly, every subject had to be pooled, washed, and thoroughly dried. No, drip-dried—we never did the concrete thinking that comes with aging. We played at talking.

"Now, now. How do you know that she's a lesbo?"

Lolly did a rather practical pirouette, her voice dancing. "Takes one to know one . . ."

Lovingly demoniac. I enjoyed it, egged her on, thinking I was learning. "Now cut that out."

But she had the floor. I was the peanut gallery, watching her stage a dance of the seven veils. Removing her third imaginary veil, she gave a chippy stripper's bump and grind. Her voice, an impersonation of a female impersonator: "Lesbian our way. Homo-kay?"

I stopped her on the fourth veil. "Cut! Print! Listen, *seriously*, how do you *know* that she *is?*"

Often I felt that Lolly gave herself up too readily to her wonderland. Also, when I didn't want to indulge in it, she became upset. I was suddenly the red queen snatching away her joints, or in honor of Lewis J. Carroll, her croquet mallets, of which she had oh, so many.

That time she snapped back, with a third position leading into a business like demi-plié. "Look, she's the daughter of some immigrant Pole. She's got washerlady hair, and she excels in sports . . ."

She must have noticed my unconcealed amazement that *she'd* noticed "Greta the lowly."

Fourth position. Her feet were angry. "I have eyes," she snapped.

I hadn't actually meant a double entendre when I said, "Yeah, with too much shadow," but she didn't get it anyway. A thought: if you're cruel, and the other person doesn't grasp it, then you're only cruel to yourself. The Lollys cause other people's cruelty to backfire.

She went into a mock go-go-girl frug, flirting with me. "Listen, Goodbottom, you could do with a few make-up lessons! *And* I know what you're thinking *and* I did go to gym class on Monday despite my oppressive period—I mean, it was gushing, but I didn't get a note or cut or anything—*and* she was there, sinking those baskets, ramming into all us girlies, all thick-ankled and hulking. It was like playing with Khrushchev's daughter!"

We were not amused. "Not quite. One is Russian and one's a Pole."

Lolly kissed both my cheeks. "Same difference," she said.

It wasn't right to let her get away with it. She had no mother, and fathers miss things.

"Spitz, you are a big bigot!"

"No, I'm being democratic."

"How's that?"

"Saying exactly what I think. In a democracy, you do that."

I let her get away with it.

I stopped telling the blacklist story, but I still go over it for myself once in a while. My mother got Marvin cleared because in her "beauty days" she'd carried on with a rich industrialist spook. He kept her in clothes and cosmetics and probably the finest cottage cheese that could be bought. All in return for as much nookie as he wished. Then she met Marvin. But every year the fat cat would send her his card telling her to call him collect any time. So when the trouble started she did just that. Finding out that he was more to the right than ever, she begged him to pull a few strings. He pulled, and my father got off.

About two months later, without explanation, my mother took a little trip to Detroit. She came back soon though . . . I guess he'd no longer found her attractive.

After the witch hunt and before the best seller, times were a bit lean. Oh, we weren't hurting, there was half a chicken in every pot. It just meant that Marvin bought English wool instead of cashmere and my mother went to drugstores for cosmetics instead of to department stores on Fifth Avenue. Having no heavy personal expenses, I felt nothing change.

When the book broke I knew everything changed. It wasn't one of Marvin Goodrich's best but it was his dirtiest. The recipe was foolproof: something for everyone. It had a whipper and a whippee, a necrophiliac and a hermaphrodite, a small boy who put lipstick on his dog, and a stripper who did things with crosses. And everyone bought it. It made all of the coffee tables in town. It topped every reader's fiction list for five months running. The sale price to paperbacks was funny. The movie sale was hilarious. We were suddenly stinking rich, which lends itself to comedy. People don't know what to do with themselves. Whether to buy a Lear jet, a cabin cruiser, or both. There were the interviews and talk shows and personal appearances, the letters and the fawning from people he loathed.

Daddy did keep his head, somewhat. He went whole hog on cashmere and bought me the best Freudian analyst in practice, but other than that—aside from the Indian reservation purchase—he hugged his loot.

Morty Manowitz, our accountant, was over at the house one day. A conscientious little man who gave me hammerlock embraces, exuding the worst breath that ever lived in a mouth.

"Listen, Prudie, I wanna have a little confab with ya. Got a moment?"

I sat far away from him. "Shoot."

Ugh! Foul breath, with a cigar to top it off. Straight Damon Runyon.

"What say ya 'bout all this hoopla?"

"Well, I'll tell ya, Morty, I say it's super fine. Everybody should be rich once."

"That is what is called a truth. I mean, I don't complain. It gives my business a lift too, ya know? Buy the wife a steak dinner, take in a show . . . it's better, ya know?"

"Sure, Morty, so what's the problem?"

He gave his cigar a suck and a tweedle, really intent on getting his point across. "Well . . . it's this way . . . I don't know about that Indian thing."

"It's called a reservation, Manowitz. The government took it away from its owners to give to a cousin of Con Edison and my father bought it in time to return it to the rightful owners. What, may I ask, is wrong with buying the property?"

He was into his cigar, hadn't seen my eyes yet. "Well . . . I'll put it to ya. It's a lousy investment. Same thing as buying a ghetto." He saw my eyes. "Ah, say, Prudie. When do the braces come off?"

It was pointless to have a "social" argument with him when all he wanted was to be liked. I grinned.

"Well, Morty, I'll tell ya. Spiritually, they're off. Literally, I still have three months to go."

"That'll be something, I'll tell ya. A real event. Marilyn Monroe's who you'll look like."

He was really something, Jesus! "Morty, I have dark hair!"

That didn't seem to stump him. "Well . . . without the hair then. A dead ringer—believe me when I say, a dead ringer!"

Success made Daddy unattainable. Not by choice. I had refused to feel neglected. Alone, yes; lonely, no. My "darkroom" life was at a place where I could survive without his immediate presence.

My mouth no longer looked like an appliance store, I'd started with my doctor, and I had Lolly. I could even separate the real from the unreal, which included my mother. I allowed her to take form. She slowly appeared to me as a real person who created her own unreality. Such steps I was taking! I was stuck in Freudian thought, so I had to unravel things his way.

Nate feels that there are other, more progressive schools of psychiatric thought. He wants me to look into them. At that time, however, I couldn't shop for myself.

It was close for a while there. Lolly and I, by an honest, but nutty fluke, went to the same couch. Our motto was "Friends who are shrunk together, stay together." I suppose that our two fathers, without consultation of course, had selected the very best for their *kinder*. The prank was delicious at first, but when we began to compare notes, the doctor got messed up.

I would lie there, fooling around with him. "Oh, a blue pillow today. I see, I see . . . Lolly said she had a green pillow. Why can't I have the green pillow? Is there something wrong with me that I have to have this pillow?"

And Lolly would lie there with her hair fanning out, a movie publicity shot of the pretty but disturbed teenager. She would pout and say, "The blinds are closed today. Why, Doctor, why? Does it mean that I have a long struggle before I open my mind? Why have you trapped me, or am I trapping myself? Oh, I must be able to see out. You let Prudence Goodrich see out. She says she can even see Woolworth's from here. When will I be ready to see Woolworth's, Doctor?"

Herr Doctor couldn't handle it. He arranged for Lolly to switch, explaining how it would be easier for her because she wasn't as far into the treatment. Diplomacy doesn't sit well with me. He was really saying one of two things: that I was more fucked up than she, or that he wanted to get into her pants more than he wanted to analyze her.

She left. I got down to cases.

We kept a large ceramic plate in the front hall. It was for my father's mail. During the "best-seller period" the plate was packed, mostly with checks and letters from little girls in Iowa who wanted to be in the movie. The letters didn't vary much, all hopelessly hopeful. "Dear Great White Author" or "Dear Marv," etc. Most had flawless spelling and punctuation, giving a clue that it was pushy Mama who wrote them. Little did they know that Daddy did not have casting privileges. Even though he was also writing the screenplay, he was only allowed to offer suggestions. It was his baby, but "they" sure weren't going to let him rock the whole cradle. When giant money is involved it's always "they." Way back then it really pissed me off, it still does. I mean, the "theys" of this country are all losers who win by riding on someone else. One head (literal term, man) does the work so that "they," these anonymous men, can get Lincoln Continentals out of it.

An empty plate usually meant that Daddy was on the premises. I would run down the hall screaming, "Gimme the man. I wanna see the man!"

He would emerge, looking bemused, worn, and attractive. He would hold out his palm to be slapped. "What's happening, baby?" he'd ask with Rotarian inflection.

I would throw up my hands in mock despair. "It's not happening any more. It's happenin'. Get it?"

He would shrug in mock defeat. "Nope. No soul in me. What's on your news front?"

I always took advantage of that introduction. I figured that if he wanted to hear, he had some time. Never lip service, never head games. When he was pressed, he'd say, "Things look good with you, right?" And I'd know that he hadn't even looked.

He'd taken me into his den that day, so I'd planned on a half an hour. My room only had a twenty-minute limit. The den was sacred. Nobody went in there when he wasn't home. The key of his wrath kept us out. He would sense organically, no matter how stealthily it was done, that the room had been entered. My mother sent the maid in once to clean it out. He left her for two months and cut off all her charge accounts. To invade that room was to deal with an "in patient."

Actually, you couldn't walk straight through if you wanted to. The Collier Brothers would have been pleased to see it. Years of literary clutter, stacks of bits and pieces. Daddy referred to it as "his mind."

They had given a cocktail party. Daddy had one too many, and opening the den door, had said to a very sharp lady editor, "Won't you come into my mind?"

To which she'd replied, "I fear, without my walking shoes, it would be too much of an undertaking."

So sitting in "his mind" that day, we caught up on things.

"Your work is the Word, isn't it?"

That little muscle that all good men of character have in their jaws flexed. "Well, let's just say that shit travels faster than diamonds."

I thought he needed opening up. "What makes you say that? Don't you like it?"

Most people just don't need you when you need

to be needed. My father lived in an isolation booth where few knocked. I did, and he welcomed it.

He gave my at that time still plump hand a squeeze. "Sure I do. It's my best friend right now. What I don't like are the reasons for it being that way. Do you follow me?"

I nodded assertion, and then guessed. "You sold out. Right?"

He looked pleased. "Right. And then I was able to cash in. Should have reread *Dr. Faustus* before I picked up my pen. Twenty-five years of writing and thinking the way I wanted to. Then I turn out something that goes against my grain and everyone congratulates me. I don't get it."

I took a cushion and hugged it. "Pleasure-pain," I said.

Marvin gaped at his sprouting *Wunderkind.* "How do you know about that?"

"I don't," I said knowingly.

My half hour was up. I didn't move. Daddy did. He grabbed the cushion from a startled me and began to sway with it, poking his thumb in his mouth. He was being playful. It never came off when he got like that. He wasn't the fey "slide down my rain barrel" type. When he stuck to his Leslie Howard stance he was safe, and so was everyone else. He put too much effort into being light-hearted. Laughing perfunctorily, I waited for his seizure of shenanigans to pass. It did. He handed the cushion back, saying wistfully, "I swear on every tax dollar that I shall never have a case of the cutes in your presence again. Now it's your turn. Talk to me."

I had nothing to say. Yes I did. "Well, I was just thinking that I have nothing to say."

His forehead broke into wrinkles in an effort to zero in on number one daughter. "That you think is important."

"Yes. But . . . I could be persuaded."

He packed his pipe. I was good for another hour. A pipe indicated that he was about to settle down and relax. Better still, he poured himself a Scotch without water. It had seemed to be my once-a-year day. For a moment I'd even considered that I had a fatal disease and he was giving himself lots of time to break it to me. I'm cautious by instinct. When a hand is offered, I select only one finger but hang on with a death grip. Nate understands. He only holds my fingers. I can't give out my hand yet.

"Do you want a drink, baby?" The great equalizer.

"Sure. Hit me with a Virgin Mary."

Daddy took a can of tomato juice out of the miniature fridge. He did a fancy mixing job in the cocktail shaker. I took a puff on the pipe and a sip of his Scotch.

"Here ya go. Watch out, it's a killer."

I took a gulp. Nothing. The dangerous kind, like they serve at South Sea restaurants. You think it's a soft drink, and after putting away two of them, you get up and fall down.

I took a few more sips. "Daddy, there's nothing cooking in here. It's just doctored tomato juice. What's the big idea?"

"It was your idea. You ordered a Virgin Mary."

"So?"

An upper-hand laugh. "Obviously, you don't know what that is. It's straight tomato juice with a shot of tabasco and Worcestershire. Non-boozers or ex-boozers order it in social situations to avoid saying 'I'll have a glass of V-8 juice' or 'No, thanks, I'm on the wagon.' "

Marvin had a way of turning a faux pas into simple misinformation.

"What a jerk-off!" I said with all the aplomb of trying out a tough term for the first time.

"Who?" asked the dashing middle-aged owl.

"Oh, some friend of Carlton's that Lolly made

me go out with. She's always trying to bring me out, but I go right back in again. She does her best."

I should have registered his expression. I should have noticed my mother. He handed me his drink. "What about the one who ordered the Virgin Mary?"

The Scotch seemed to course into my breasts. I transported myself to a room filled with moving mouths, smoke, and traveling canopies. I was wearing something small and black, with one "good fake" diamond earring swaying on my lobe. The other had fallen into my Baccarat champagne glass. It was all so amusing and I did so love everybody, and there was Lolly across the room looking so mousy. I answered the attentive fellow next to me who'd asked a question. "Well, he did it like he was asking for a weapon, and *then* he had the nerve to pretend to get sloshed. I *mean*, he didn't even have an ID."

Back to the den. Marvin milked the subject. "What did you have?"

"A Coke. I forgot to borrow Lolly's fake proof. It's hard to be getting older and have these legal phantoms dictate that you're still a youngster. What is it that the nymphet says in your book?"

He chuckled with fatherly pride, as though someone had cooed at an ugly baby. "She says 'I'm old enough to be your daughter.' I can just see it—in twenty years some prof at an eastern college saying 'Class, please turn to page forty-three in your Goodrich' . . . But you know, you kids do make it hard on yourselves."

I'd looked at him in disbelief. "What kind of a prig Victorian statement is that?"

He put out his pipe. "Nothing, Prude. Forget it, huh? I just want you to enjoy a glass of tomato juice once in a while."

For whatever reason, tears were waiting. "I do, really. Tomato juice has always been a personal favorite."

I was eager for dismissal, when Daddy poured another Scotch. "So, what else is doing?" He asked in a way that required any old answer.

I was having a struggle for control. I couldn't imagine why. It had to do with Daddy's subtext, but I couldn't get at it. "Nothing much." I pouted.

He gargled a swig of his drink. "Come on now, spit it out."

"I don't want to. I do that at the doctor's."

"How is the doctor, by the way?"

"Oh, he's coming along quite nicely. Sends his best."

Daddy looked puzzled at my sudden demon

streak. I decided to stop being huffy. "No, I really don't have any idea how he is but I'm getting better. We're into dreams now."

"Good sign. Are yours loaded?"

I was the teacher. "All dreams are loaded. Especially the ones you can't remember. The first sign of trouble is when you say you don't dream. That indicates that you're blocking off the subconscious to hide your uglies."

He seemed impressed. "Well, in that case, I dream straight through the night! I even wake up out of breath in the morning."

I had this fierce burning sensation around the left breast area. It was one out of three: a psyche figment, my heart, or the Scotch. I tried to brave it out. "Oh, Marv . . . you're putting me on. You wake up short of breath because you smoke too much. You don't remember a thing. You sleep like a baby, which means you're really in the danger zone."

He took a playful swat at me. I grabbed his hand, making him hug me. "Maybe I should go now. I have homework."

He kept on hugging me. "Just one more thing, baby."

My head was embedded in his sweater. "What?" I couldn't see his face. It might have been affection that had us locked in embrace, but he made it almost impossible for me to look at him.

His voice was fogged. "They're going to start casting the movie soon."

I turned my head to the side. "Oh, 'they' are, are 'they'?"

He turned up his volume. "Yes. And as you know, the young girl is a very pivotal role."

I had a vague sixth sense, so I stayed in his sweater. "And you want me to play it," I muffled.

He tightened his grip. "She can't have brown hair."

I was clinging to him. "So I'll dye it."

He dropped his arms, moving back, but I kept my position, my face turned away to the side.

The room was too still for two people who were in the same family. So maybe this was the "gap." But Marvin would always reach me. "No," he said flatly, "Your hair's too pretty to ruin it . . ."

"A wig."

"No. She can't go through the whole picture with a wig on."

For the first time we were psychologically jousting. "Get to the point, man!" I hadn't realized that I'd yelled until I saw his neck muscles bulge.

"I want them to see Lolly. Maybe test her."

The two of them snowplowing, chair-lifting, rope-towing, yodeling into the sunset. . . .

It had been hard for him, but I needed to make it harder. "Because *she's* pretty."

He spoke with such careful tenderness that I could barely hear him. "Yes, she is. So are you. But she's closer to the physical concept, that's all. She's got the blond hair which they think is essential. The next time I'll write a screenplay just for you."

I sucked in my cheeks, widening my eyes, trying to keep the tears out. "Ya, sure. She'll make such a big hit in this one that you'll break ass to get her for the next."

He smiled without his eyes. "They haven't even seen her yet."

I tickled my palms, trying to keep those tears out. "If I'm your baby all the time, how come I don't win?"

I walked to the bar, pouring an elephant glass of Scotch. At the door, I couldn't turn around. My face was all wet. "I'll have her call you," I said.

Lolly must have seen about it. Nothing was mentioned, though, for about two weeks. I treated my father politely, which was unheard of between us.

During the third week of undercurrents I asked Lolly when she'd signed her contract and whether she'd be shooting in Hollywood or New York, and what her going price would be for her next picture. We'd been sitting in Schrafft's, gorging on butterscotch sundaes.

She looked incredulous, stopping frozen, her spoon halfway to her mouth. "What was that?"

Good little piece of acting. The drama coaches must have started shaping her up. "Also, you won't be able to eat sundaes like normal people any more. Camera puts ten pounds on you."

"What are you babbling about, Prude? I don't have the foggiest idea what you mean."

She was too polished. It had to be real. "The movie. Aren't you going to be in Daddy's movie?"

In a rush of passion, she leaped across the table, giving me a solid buss on the cheek. "Boy, are you an ass. Who would be the first person I'd tell?"

"I dunno, your analyst. Well, you kept quiet for a while, like movie stars with big deals before the public announcement, so I figured that it was in the bag. Why, didn't you get it?"

She'd finished her ice cream, starting in on the rolls. They put a bread basket on the tables, no matter what, even if you order an Alka-Seltzer.

"Um . . . They didn't think I was right."

"That's impossible! You *are* what Daddy wrote. They didn't even read you or test you?"

Something was bewildering me. Something was not quite ordinary. It was like staring at one of those magazine contests where they have as a title over a drawing "What's Wrong with This Picture?" After much mulling, and feeling doltish, you discover that the lady's profile is minus a nostril.

Lolly buttered her second roll. I watched her abstractedly. "Well, I'm going to have Daddy tell the men to call you back because . . ."

"No! Don't!" She'd reacted like Barbara Stanwyck in peril.

"Why?" I asked, perfectly guileless, because I was.

"I lied. I called your father and he'd wanted to meet with me first. I guess to see if I'd developed a ghastly case of acne or something."

The truth was not present. In a way that I didn't understand, I was being conned. I said, "He could have asked me."

Third roll; no butter.

"Ya, but he said you weren't speaking to him. Anyhow . . . I met with him and . . ."

"Where?"

"Prudence, really! We went to Sardi's. *Très* fun. Anyhoo, he said he'd mulled it over and he really didn't think I should meet anyone because it would disrupt my school year, my friendship with you, and possibly my life. He kept saying he didn't want 'them' to get hold of me."

My mind had seemed to be racing past my thoughts. "What did you have?"

"Where, sleuth?"

"At Sardi's. What did you eat?"

"Who ate? I had a whiskey sour straight up, with extra cherries."

The inflection she gave "cherries" made me settle down. She said it like a little kid.

"Why did you have a drink? They have such good food. You should have had shrimp à la Sardi."

"I know. My stomach was growling like mad. But I once heard this woman say, in a bluesy voice, 'I'll just drink my dinner.' So I tried to be sophisticated. I mean, I was with an older man. When I start to eat, I get messy."

I hadn't touched my sundae. "Did you see any famous folk?"

She started gathering her books together. "Nah. Only your father."

I woke up at four in the morning. Lolly never ate breadstuffs. She said they were bad for the digestive system. In all the years I'd known her, she'd never taken a roll. Great mystery title: *The Carbohydrate Guilt.*

A few Saturday's ago I went to the zoo with Nate. He's a real buff, knows the animals' schedules by heart. He'd once traveled to a zoo in Fort Worth, Texas, just to see a breed of extinct mammal that had been scientifically re-created. He maintains that natural animals are the first wonder of the world. I once saw him almost strike a little boy who was feeding an elephant pizza.

I had arrived early at the seals. We usually met there at twelve noon. We'd watch them get fed, barking, ducking, and grinning when they caught a morsel. Nate says that seals have Jewish backgrounds. They know how to enjoy.

Then we'd go to the cafeteria and select the most remote table. We'd feed each other, pretending to be seals. Once a very intense fellow came over to us, asking if we wanted to join his acting class. When we declined, he said that he'd *really* enjoyed watching us and that we *really* knew how to relate.

That Saturday, waiting by the pond for him, I got a natural high. I wanted to thank all the strangers around me. A young couple next to me tossed their

Cracker Jack boxes into the pond. I felt sad for them. People just don't know what to do with their clutter.

There he was. Paper under his arm, brown corduroy suit, beige turtleneck sweater, one hand free to take mine.

"Look at their water today, Spitz! It's filthy. The seals aren't at all happy."

Try to locate a zookeeper these days. It's like trying to find a cop when you really need one. We eventually spotted one by the yaks.

Nate took over. "When was the seal water last changed?"

The zookeeper shrugged.

"Do you like your job?"

Another shrug.

"Check the water thing out, will you? Jobs are pretty scarce at the moment."

After we'd walked away, I asked him, "Are you going to come back on Monday to find out if he did it?"

"You bet your sweet I am."

Nate is a man of contrasts. He's very rich but is deeply affected by very simple things. Perhaps, though, had he been poor, he wouldn't have been able to afford to care.

After lunch we'd walked down Fifth Avenue

looking at the shops. I called it window shoplifting. Materialistic bitch that I am, I would mentally take everything that caught my eye. We'd strolled along, holding fingers, occasionally stopping at some splashy display. He had that rueful look again.

"I feel like a tourist, Prude."

"Oh no, never! Saturday people are the natives. Sunday people are the tourists."

We were in front of Mark Cross. I was staring at a smart-looking briefcase made out of pigskin.

"Do you like that, Puss?"

He'd jolted me. The case had reminded me of Lolly, who was always gathering up one too many books. "Nope, I don't like it particularly."

Lolly's total absence in our togetherness suddenly depressed me. "How's Lol?" I tried in abbreviating her name to sound casual.

But he stiffened at the mere mention of "the other woman" in his life. "Why?" he asked, perusing the window intently.

"Because I know she'd like the gift you just offered me, because I don't get around much any more with her, and because since you just acted defensive, I guess you know about as little as I do."

"We meet at the refrigerator," he said sadly, "and discuss what we're about to snack on."

By the time we stopped at Scribner's window, the subject of Lolly had receded, and we were just an extraordinary couple once again. He did his usual offering bit. "You see anything you'd like to read? If not, don't waste Mr. Scribner's time."

Nate was attentive to my likes and dislikes, never wasting his money on an item that I was only lukewarm about.

Once, spoofing a loaded old sugar Daddy, he asked, "Baby, ya want the Taj Mahal?"

I'd nodded, licking an imaginary lollipop.

"Then, baby, you got it . . . C.O.D."

We'd passed the Museum of Modern Art, tempted but not willing to fight the crowds and get slugged with cameras. We'd jaunted along, not saying much, sharing smiles, sporadically playing our food game.

"Nate, quick! Eggs Benedict with too much hollandaise."

"Well, maybe to you. To me, she's pure Welsh Rarebit."

Nate was by far the better player.

"Hey, did you see her?"

"Who, Puss?"

"That blond number that just walked by us?"

"No. I didn't."

I physically felt his mood swing. "Would you have looked at her with appreciation if you had seen her?"

"Probably not."

"You're an odd duck sometimes."

"I agree with you. I am."

"If I ask you something, will you answer it?"

He almost allowed himself to laugh at my illogic. "I won't know until you ask it."

I looked right into his eyes, which is technically impossible, but the effect can be achieved by directing your focus to the center of the nose. I thought it most alluring, but Nate told me later that he'd been worried about my vision.

"Do you play around?"

"No."

"Why not?"

"No interest."

His attitude was grim, like it had been that first afternoon in his office. It made me uneasy. It was so unpredictable that I couldn't decide whether I'd provoked it.

"I know the bit. Your interest lies in your business."

He corrected me. "My interest used to be solely in my work."

People seemed to be detouring around us.

"I'm very important to you, aren't I?"

"Very." He'd confirmed it.

I slipped my whole hand in his and we walked on.

Lolly began to thaw in May of our senior year. We hadn't spoken for over four months and I'd stopped watching for signs. Our estrangement had bound me closer to her father, which had taken me away from my own.

Once I had a bird that died. I thought I'd never get over it. The next day I was given a turtle. Different species, different relationship, but such comfort in the possibility of replacement.

When we met, I'd usually ask Nate about how his daughter was doing. He would look a bit sheepish. "Probably not as well as you are, Puss. I think she misses you."

But if she did, I wasn't able to get to her to find out. Early in the feud I'd considered calling and asking her doctor if she discussed me, but that would have made me less than an "honorable man." I was already Brutus enough.

She'd made herself scarce, forming a whole new life. At school she was omnipresent as ever, still the leader of the rat pack. The most popular girl in our grade. I was regarded with a certain respect by her friends because they thought that I'd deliberately broken away from her Svengali influence. I suppose nobody really likes popularity that much if they are without it.

College fever permeated the last quarter of the school year. There wasn't much room for camaraderie or petit-point gossip.

I'd had the preliminary formal conference about application way back in January. You had to have one, preferably both, parents present. I brought Marvin, of course, because Mummy would have slept through it.

The clubwoman type on the administration who interviewed us gushed a bit over Daddy's book and then dove into the nitty-gritty. She'd said, rather dubiously, that I was certainly bright enough to get into any one of the "seven sister" colleges. However, she'd felt, after looking at the total picture (meaning my hangups, "problem child" syndrome again), that I'd be more at ease, more suited, to one of the slightly avant-garde (loony bin) campuses. She gave us both a list, asking if there were any questions.

I piped up. "Are these dives all co-ed?"

With professional hard-core finesse she told me that usually the off-beat colleges were. Then, with a blush and a whinny, she said that most sanctioned complete cohabitation but that she was sure I would avoid the hedonistic tendencies of higher learning. I understand why many older ladies nix sex. It's because they haven't gotten any lately.

She asked Marvin if he had any opinions, to which he replied in style. "Well, I can give you a first-hand account of universities. I attended an excellent one. It's called life."

Being drummed in the psychology of dealing with problem parents as well, she said that he'd obviously graduated sigma cum laude.

In the hall, on our way to the elevators, we'd passed Lolly and her father. The two men nodded briefly.

"I'm going to hijack you for a couple of minutes," my father said when we reached the ground floor.

"It's against the rules." I grinned my approval. "We have an obligatory graduation practice, and there's a little deli down the street that has the best pastrami on rye and barrel-style pickles in the history of the New Testament."

I seldom gave him steers about food. Marvin reverently ate his sandwich and most of mine. But we weren't there for the pleasure of his palate. He felt his pockets. "So you think you're college material?"

"Why, does Ohrbach's need salesgirls?" I snapped it, annoyed at the pastrami grease on his chin, doubly annoyed that I thought I could afford to be fresh. His eyes flashed a "don't forget who you're talking to." I decided to flip the subject. "They have a fair cherry cheese cake here. It's not made on the premises, you can tell by the crust, but at least it's cream cheese and doesn't taste like phlegm."

He registered no interest in confections. "Can you catch me up on the subject of one Mr. Spitz as succinctly as you've caught me up on cheese cake?"

I still adulated my father, but at that moment I intensely disliked the Marvin Goldfarb that my mother got every day of her life. A man who let you be, and let you completely alone so that you *had* to be, and then, without warning, zeroed in on privates. And yet he had an omnipotent quality that made everything his business. I had no choice.

In a clerical fashion, I itemized: "He calls me Puss; I do not call him Boots. There is nothing cutesy or servant-master about us. At first he was the sun and the moon and the stars because of the special effects of his 'older mandom.' Now he's just the day, which makes him a fantastic reality. I wake up and think Nate, not B+ on a chem paper. I go to sleep thinking Nate, not is so-and-so going to ask me to the hop. He's rescued me from being my age, which I never was good at anyway . . . Hello?"

Marvin was drumming on the table like men do who are bored with their wives and having sexual fantasies about their mistresses. He looked up, giving the deli man the signal, check. To me, he said, icily cozy, "I'm sure your time with him is well spent."

"Oh, it most certainly is. We quilt, glaze clay in the old kiln—projects, projects," I said in high cunt style, and then, quickly with an eraser, "Oh, Daddy, let's not be average about this and lousy to each other."

Marvin expanded. "I just want you to have a normal education," he said with a cornball smile that alarmed me.

"Well, so does he," I said, wishing that I didn't have to betray myself by sounding so mundane.

• • •

I'd applied, nonchalantly, to several of the colleges on my list. I filled out the multiple forms with determined disrespect. Religious preference: Buddhist; sex: uncertain; health: failing rapidly, etc. My powers of concentration were invested in Nate.

When I'd visit him in the evenings, Lolly was never home. He said that she usually arranged to spend the night with David, her latest, or a friend. A typical Victorian household!

Lately I'd felt the strain of Lolly's absence in Nate. It wasn't the kind of loss of "she's grown up before my very eyes," but rather "where is she doing her growing up, and with whom?" I knew Lolly was accommodating me by not being there, yet she was also punishing her father. I never went into her room; I had no right to. I also felt I had no right to even talk about her, which was wrong. It was no way to resolve things.

We'd just finished what I called a "married people's dinner," and what he called "eating sensible." We'd had lamb chops, beets, baked potato, salad, and Jello. Nothing to make love on. Ever since I'd arrived, we'd been in a rut of friendly behavior. I wanted sparks. "There has to be a resolution," I said, interrupting one of the President's State of the Union messages.

"Not with this administration," Nate said grimly.

He'd misunderstood me but had given a comprehensive answer. I should have let it go, poured him another cup of Sanka, and been glad that he took an interest in nutrition, the affairs of state, and me. "No, I meant with Lolly."

"Oh," he said without inflection. He walked over and turned the set off. "The President was talking so loud I couldn't hear you. Excuse him. What about her?"

He seemed less evasive. I asked, "Just how is she, in specific?"

He took out a bottle of crème de menthe (to make up for the lamb chops; touch time, after all). "She seems to be coming around. I gather that some older fella gave her a rough inning, but she's friendlier, so maybe it's over. She came into the den this morning, gave me a kiss, and we talked for a while. She seemed relieved."

I felt, listening to him, that an example was being cited. "Is that the criterion for relief? That something's over?"

He soothed what he didn't even know scared me. "Sure. For those who can't handle the problem."

The crème de menthe worked my way onto his lap. "Where did she kiss you?"

He pointed to his cheek.

"I'll do one better," I said, suddenly possessive.

• • •

I had been shocked at the collection of fat envelopes I'd received. The tradition goes that skeleton envelopes mean a college rejection. Fat envelopes mean you're in, kid. I had five bids out of six, and the sixth had been the only one question marked on the list, anyway. Jesus! The others must have really had to fill their quota of "sickies."

The day following an unusually loving night at Nate's, I walked out of school, coatless and blithe. I'd been chatting with Naomi in front of the gate. She'd looked full blown and almost peppy.

"So, Nai, are you going to Bennington? Did you accept their scholarship?"

Like Ariel in *The Tempest,* she'd laughed and danced around. "No, no, no, no."

"Why?" I knew that she'd worked her tranquillity off to get in.

"Because I've had an interruption. I'm pregnant."

"Oh Jesus, no!"

"But this time I'm having it. It's wonderful. He really loves me now, and we're going to live together somewhere."

I was about to bless her when I noticed Lolly walking alone up the block, wearing a blazer and scarf. It was sundress weather. "Listen, Nai, can't talk now —I'll call you tonight."

I galloped up the street to catch Lolly before the light changed. Somehow I knew that she'd be approachable.

As I reached her, panting, she giggled. "Oh, Prude, you're too skinny to be so out of breath."

We eyed each other carefully, like old lovers who had been reunited. She'd never mentioned my figure before. I'd never noticed that she was really quite beautiful.

"Ya. Well, I . . ."

"Well nothing. You smoke like a fiend. My dear old dad's influence on the young."

I heard no bitterness, and her eyes had "forgive" in them.

"But aside from that, you look fantastic! A before and after that worked. I told you that you'd be a looker."

I refused to allow her to do a snow job. I wanted to make my points. Although we seemed to resume our normal course, we hadn't yet. She was guilty until proven guilty.

"I thank you, my mother thanks you, my father thanks you. Oh, and your father thanks you. Now. How have you been? Why didn't your man of the moment call for you at school today, a Friday? *And* why, pray, are you bundled up for the north winds? You've got three minutes or you lose the trip to Niagara Falls."

She gave this gutsy laugh that I didn't know she had in her. I'd heard about how people change but I'd always taken it to mean for the worse.

She was Tinker Bellish as hell, and everyone who knows their James M. Barrie will concede that Tinker Bell was quite a dame. Lolly didn't seem as "knowing," but much more genuine.

"Okay, okay. If it's not Atlantic City, I don't want to go anyway. First question again, please."

"How have you been?"

"Lots of changes, Prude. Next?"

"Sorry. You'll have to be more specific. What changes?"

"You always were a bug on details."

"Ya. Well, they make up what goes on. Are you going to answer the question?"

She was weighing. "Eventually. Hey, let's go somewhere and sit. Only hookers stand on a corner this long."

I must have hesitated. She touched my arm very lightly. "Do you have time, or don't you want to, or are you meeting my father?"

I glanced down without reason. She was carrying the pigskin briefcase.

"Yes to the first, and the other two don't matter right now."

We decided against a cocktail lounge because we wanted to talk our age and not pose as older just to get a drink, which would be skimpy of booze anyway, because whoever waited on us would know we were younger.

We ended up at a coffee shoppee where they had Danish that you could use for ammunition. We both, spontaneously, ordered milk.

"God, Prude! Have we ever grown down!"

I took out my pigskin cigarette case. I think it startled her.

"Mark Cross?"

"Yup. What about your briefcase?"

"Yes, as a matter of irony."

The clues were in orbit. Now wishing to appear the fool, I proceeded with caution. This ship, I was going to run.

"Okay. We'll skip to the second question. Why wasn't anybody squiring you up the street today?"

I was relieved that she'd chosen to be candid. Two people in analysis can really become paranoid together.

"They're all gone. I got rid of the last one about the same time I stopped speaking to you."

"Which was the same time I started making it with Nate, I mean your father. And there are no rolls on this table, Lolly."

She knew what I would eventually arrive at, or

what she would tell me, but she wasn't quite following my plan of attack.

But she was no stupe. "What does that have to do with the price of . . . fathers?"

"Two years' worth of mine, Lolly. We're playing games."

She took off her blazer. "I know we are . . . Another milk? I'll stake you."

The waitress told us that they'd run out of milk, which made us laugh, easing our tension.

"Have the last four months been happy for you, Lolly?"

Her smile was tight, contradicting her affirmative nod. I plunged ahead. "Tell me, why aren't you wearing one of your seasonal sundresses?"

"Well," she said, studying the table, "May is still a bit chilly."

It was like eating lobster. There's one claw that always resists invasion. But the bites you do get taste better than the rest. More worthwhile.

Probing into the claw again. "You're getting practical in your old age. I mean, taking care of yourself like an older person would."

The look she gave me was unforgettable. It told everything. "Prudie, don't be upset."

"I'm absolutely not."

"Yes, you are."

"I know I am."

"Prudie . . ."

"Say it!"

"Say what?"

"You say who's been making you happy for the past two years. I want to hear it out loud."

"Marvin Goodrich has."

We'd beat the system. We'd progressed further than our progressive education.

"Now you can see how I felt about you and Nate, Prude."

She sounded a shade sanctimonious, her eyes a trifle narrow for a conversation alive with revelations. She was sapping the fun out of confronting her.

"But you were doing the same thing! *You started it!*" I said, silently begging her to back out and deny everything.

"Prude, it's different when the father involved is your own. It's a real kick. A kick in the head. Now you know."

"Ya. And I thought you'd have a giggle when I told you about yours."

She seemed done with her hurt. I was still behind mine. She was in a position to comfort me. She should. She knew more about my father than I ever would. My throat constricted. "Jesus! This has got to be written up in psychiatric journals! Jesus!"

"Use your napkin, Prude."

"I don't care. I've cried over less."

The waitress, who was a black of the old school, came over to ask if anything was wrong. Lolly said that I was just having a touch of premarital difficulty.

Within five minutes the waitress was back, holding a large glass of milk. "I went to another place for it, honey. You'll need every drop you can get."

I was laugh-crying. "Lolly, you made her think I'm knocked up! I'm not even married."

"The two have nothing to do with each other."

"With Nate Spitz they do!"

"Oh, please! Why so formal? Feel free to call him my father."

She was trying to show me "wherein the humor lay." She probably wanted to discuss life in the old kip. I wasn't, never would be, up to that. Confiding with my best friend Lolly was one thing. It was quite another with my father's woman, or my man's daughter.

And marriage! Why that plebeian state had never entered my . . . yes, it had. Nate and I had left the "in all seasons an older man's fancy" stage behind. I was too young to be kept and not old enough to want to be. I wasn't exactly prize marriage stock—but then, who is? Astrologically I'm on the cusp of Cancer and Leo, with Cancer in the lead. I'm upset with every connotation of Cancer: disease, domesticity, placidity, maternal sensitivity, and a host of other dreary traits. I deny any Cancer in me, as I strike my match. Until Nate, my moon was in the wrong house, so with him, I'm a Leo.

Lolly had ordered a small salad because as soon as it gets dark, she decides it's hungry time. Our waitress was automated to bring me glass after glass of milk. Well, nice people doing crummy jobs are rare. I'd leave her a cow for a tip.

I was a bit punchy from finally cracking the case. "Did my daddy give you that briefcase?"

Eating was Lolly's occupation therapy. "Nope," she said.

"Who did?"

"My daddy."

"He did?!?"

"Now, now. He'll always be my daddy, Mrs. Spitz." She was sitting there with a milk mustache, looking twelve, suggesting the most complex thing I'd ever heard of.

"It must have entered your mind, Prude. I mean, you weren't brought up to marry the boy next door. Being Daddy's wifey occurred to you, didn't it?"

"Yes, for the two of us. But not a quartet!"

She primped at her window reflection, and as the mood struck, did a zany pantomime of playing four different musical instruments. She ended humming the Wedding March.

A little bit of fey stretches a long way. I felt prickly. "Lolly, this is serious."

Her face and body changed to "woman." "No, you're wrong. It's beautifully funny and touchingly sincere and marvelously mad and very much *us*. Don't make it grotesque for yourself. You're apt to do that, you know. Old Carlton once said that you could be wonderful if you didn't think you were so terrible. I happen to be in love with a man who happens to be your father, and vice versa. So what's so confusing? It's very mathematical."

I could see Marvin with her. She was always very ripe because she gave just what she could every moment. Never indulging, but moving on to the next handout. She would be an excellent breast-feeder.

"Did you tell the Doc, Lol?"

"Um. I'm not going to be with him much longer."

"Why?"

"He says he only deals with single people's problems."

I knew what Nate meant by hearing and listening. At first I'd only heard what she'd said. "What? *What?*"

"What, what? Prude?"

"What you said! You said something about losing your singlehood. He asked you. Did he ask you? Did my father ask you to marry him?"

She was most calm. I was most jealous. I felt left behind.

"Eventually we'll get married."

"When's eventual?"

"When the divorce goes through."

"You mean my mother?"

This was insane. She was telling me about the breakup of my own home. I wanted to bite her. To get back at her for feeling the same things that I did. "Lolly, how did your mother really die?"

She put her blazer on in slow motion.

"Ask Daddy about it. He'll tell you."

I didn't want to bite her any more. "Lolly, that's just it! That's the cleaner's bag. That's why he can't get over to me."

She got out of the booth. Now she was a "registered nurse" . . . bedpan, catheter . . . very starched.

"Lolly . . ."

No nonsense. The patient must rest.

"Prudie, he loves you. He's very, very in love with you. Don't be a baby."

There was no flamboyance in the way Nate cared about me. No rash statements of passionate eternity. Declarations are selfish. I mistrust the affections of someone who's on a "do you realize how much I love you?" bender. Those are the kind who burn themselves with cigarettes. Too tortured.

Nate once said, after we'd had rampant sex, that the physical love one feels must come from the heart. I had gently twanged his thingy. "How 'bout him?"

"Easily explained. Instead of our friend the heart sending a message to the brain right off, it takes a detour."

He'd explained everything but himself to me. He seemed to be programed for disappointment even though I'd never let him down in obvious ways, like not meeting him under the Biltmore clock. But he had a protection. It was as if he'd just called for himself at the cleaner's and hadn't removed that annoying transparent covering they put on.

Nate had been gung ho about college for me. (Actually, I'd dropped out of college before I ever went. It was as if I'd been holding out for alternative higher education.)

"Why? I'm not your son who should go to Yale just like the old man did."

"It was Princeton and I feel you should go."

"To Princeton. Ya. Right. I'm one hell of a quarterback."

"No. Choose the most appetizing campus on your list and start packing."

"Are you trying to get rid of me?"

"Yes, my love."

"I choose the University of Alaska."

"Awfully cold . . ."

"Again. Are you trying to get rid of me?"

"Yes. But stick around the New York State area, just in case."

His attitude of "go, girl" fed my attitude of "not on your ass."

"Okay, Spitz, give me the finite reason for going!"

He handed me a cigarette. "To major in malapropism."

I stubbed out the freshly lit cigarette. "What's that?"

Methodically he relit the cigarette, handing it to me again. "First you should go to find out what it means, and then major in it. The word means misuse of the language, Puss. You see, you should go to broaden yourself."

That pat little bit of philosophy made me hoppin' mad. "What a crock! What a crock of ca ca! Oh, and I didn't malaprop, that's Ionesco's word for shit! . . . Yeah, you get broad. In the hips, because you stuff your face the whole time because you're frustrated because you can't be with the one person *you* want to be with because *he* wants you to be there!"

He flinched. I'd won!

"What about N.Y.U.?" he asked.

I'd lost.

That night I had a short dream. An epigram: Lolly rode my father to school. I rode him back.

Short, but far from sweet. I woke up wet. I had questions that weren't rhetorical. My mind could stretch only so far; my analyst could take it only so much farther.

Farther. Freudian whoopsie. So close to *Father*. What had Lolly done with my father? How much had been returned? I wanted to go back to sleep and dream of a key that would open up doors. I threw back the covers to let myself dry. Remind Nate to buy rubber sheets in case of bad nightmares.

"What kind of nightmares, Puss?"

"Oh, ones about your daughter riding my father."

Never. Nate wasn't geared to the psyche. He knew where his meat was, where his vegetables were, and where his baked potatoes with sour cream and chives was. And he knew where I was. Everyone else played tag but Nate. The finest part of our relationship was that we stopped each other from galloping away. I felt like a question box. Was he neglecting Lolly? By the same token, was Marvin overlooking me? A kid should never start with "Daddy, why is the sky blue?" in the first place. But the question that bothered me most was the least selfish. Was my father done with Lolly, and was she bluffing to keep up with me, the former lightweight underdog? Dear Lolly, to thine own self be flirty and sexy, but true. Dear Marvin, I realize that you can't be the whole Trinity, but choose one of them.

I decided that school wasn't for me the next day. I took three Empirins but the dream refused to move out of my head. I had a malady called "The Violets." A combination of the blues and the mean reds. After my reconciliation with Lolly, I felt more estranged from her than when she'd exiled me. The peace pipe we had smoked left me with nicotine poisoning. Or out-growing pains? I'd never inhaled on the peace pipe, not really down to the gut. I'd watched her, listened to her, hoped for belief, but I never inhaled.

Dear, dear Lolly, I'm taking your father, but you can't have mine because he doesn't . . . wait—hurry—stop—go!

I went. To the door of Marvin's "mind." Closed. I couldn't. He was the creator. Of what? Me. He was also just a guy who'd screwed my best friend and written a dirty book. My fist went up . . . and came down. I couldn't.

Where do you go when you've cut school and no one sends you to your room? Out. I took my umbrella, I needed some rain.

A gen-u-ine sparkler was the great outdoors. The Irish, on St. Patrick's Eve, pray for such a day. I felt like a bit of a tourist ass, bumbling along with my bumbershoot. It wasn't a tuck-in-the-crook folding travel kind either. It was a large, happily striped "see I'm a smartie and prepared" kind.

Where to go? I had the whole city, which means nothing to a native. New York is a marvel for people who aren't miserable, which eliminates most of the dwellers. I mean, the majority of New Yorkers are minorities who, with the great city at their feet, kick it. They take it out on New York when they can't take it in any more. "Up all of your giggys" flash the neon signs if you stand on your head—and you're Puerto Rican.

I had my phone money and enough left over for

a drink. What better, on a whitewash day, for a hookey-playing, seventeen going on eighteen, maybe about to be married to a much older man, girl to do.

I had been walking steadily for twenty minutes. It was eleven-thirty in the morning. A drink, a little old pick-me-up, was out of the question. Too sad. Coffee-black (with plenty of cream 'n' sugar) was a close second.

I took the Lexington Avenue bus down to 57th Street, where there is a coffee shop that serves coffee in giant mugs that don't have chips on their rims. They also give free refills and the waitresses let you sit and smoke a half a pack without getting pushy. I've sent them a lot of fifteen-cent business. They know me there but let me remain anonymous. They never say, "Hiya, hon."

I studied my set of bus people. Mostly Republican-Unitarian. One important Democrat, Arthur Schlesinger, Jr., sat alone in a double seat, unnoticed. Bus people differ from taxi takers—less money, more character. My father never took the bus. He said he wanted to. He'd say "Let's bus it today," but then he'd want to hail one. You don't hail a bus.

"Oh, excuse me, I'm terribly, frightfully, terribly sorry."

An elderly lady had tripped on my umbrella

stem. She would make a stink, I saw it coming in her jowls. I got up quickly, to placate, offering her my seat. Glaring, she took it. A silent exchange—until she got herself all settled, all coiled up.

"It's not even raining," she hissed.

I now understand the arbitrary murder motive.

The coffee was good. I had two cups black and the third, café au lait. I'd killed fifteen minutes. I was stalling . . . maybe a little something in the stomach . . . nah, not a place for eating . . . a farm breakfast on a farm . . . who had a farm? . . . brunch at a snazzy *dolce vita* place where the women wear designer clothes . . . Mama wore label clothes but she could never make it up for brunch . . . that lady on the bus would get hers. I said *I was sorry* . . . those three words, probably the most ignored in the whole U.S. . . . Daddy to Lolly, "I am sorry" . . . Mr. Aurbach to Lolly, "Sorry" . . . The man next to me ate his sausages with Nazi ferocity . . . Nazis to Jews, "Und ve are sorry!" . . .

The first two of New York's finest phone booths on the corner smelled of urine and were out of order. The third smelled of urine but functioned at last when I put in a quarter (a phone booth with rich blood). I panicked for a moment when I heard the dial tone, forgetting his number. I closed my mind, letting my finger automatically do the dialing. If he was in there, he never let it ring more than once.

"Goodrich."

"Hello, Daddy."

Silence, because I'd broken his. He'd been "creating."

"Prudence here, Daddy."

Shock of recognition. "Oh! Hi! You on your lunchtime?"

"In a way. I'm not at school. I didn't go today . . ." It had to come up. I had to vomit it up. Let him do the digesting.

"Prudence? You okay?"

"No. But I'll be better if you answer something for me. You owe it to me, in a way, because I'm involved. I mean, it's not like I'm digging into your personal life. It was my personal life first. Shit! Can I shoot, Daddy?"

His voice came in fast. "Shoot."

"You and Lolly are having a big thing, aren't you?"

Sledge-hammered into the receiver. "No."

"Daddy, don't be obstinate. You had it, it lasted two years, and it's over, right?" Jesus, he was lousy quiz-game material. "Daddy, the quarter's running down. Just tell me. Please, I need it *out!*"

And one, two cha-cha-cha . . .

On the fourth cha, he answered. "We were involved, as they say in melodramas. We are not any more."

"When were you?"

I heard by his sigh that I was being trying. I should have just mailed in my questionnaire.

He used the voice reserved for my mother. "Do you want me to give you the exact dates?"

I used the voice reserved for my mother. "No. I don't have a pencil handy . . . I'm sorry."

He was too. "Prudence, it's over, believe me."

Good-bye, Lolly. We both had a very nice time . . .

"Thank you, Daddy. I'll see you later." I hung up, leaving him to cope.

I sat down in the phone booth, making sure the seat didn't have anything peculiar on it. Soon the trembling stopped. I looked out and up—not a cloud in the sky. The next call would be easier . . .

"Nate? Come and get me."

A soft belch. He'd just eaten lunch. The businessman's special. "Where are you?"

Everything toppling for a moment. "I don't know."

"Yes you do."

"You're right . . . I'm calling from the third urinal at 57th and Lex."

Easy laugh. "I know the one. I'll be right down. Don't get your feet wet, Puss."

"I won't."

"Hang tight. I'll be there."

"I will. I know. 'Bye."

I went outside to wait for him. Pushing the umbrella up, I held it, covering me, at full mast.

Four days later my mother got the white-coat treatment. She picked up on her exit line, and her timing was a director's dream. The sad thing was that she had no role left any more. It was as if we were all "play doctors" who had written her part out. It just had to go, better for the play. Snip. Better for the cast, healthier characters, firmer relationships. Snip. Budget expenses down, a faster curtain call, relief backstage, cozier in the dressing rooms. I mean, we had a goddamn hit on our hands! *If* Lolly had been believed. Since I chose to honor the word of my father, I grieve for the loss of both Lolly and my mother.

And everyone took it so well. Gone but forgotten. No mourning, no keening. It was better than death, cleaner. Oh, they all hoped for recovery, but at a future date, too far in advance to plan for. They didn't want to see it. They didn't want to say "So glad you're back." They didn't want to care. I'm not name-calling. It was my mother who lost the mind. She should do the name-calling.

I wonder what it feels like to leave your mind. Peaceful, maybe. I guess the mind goes to a position where there is no wondering about rational fears like that. And it's always over some horror that no one else can see. A shopping list. The safe people say "I'm simply going out of my mind." It's said in fun, said with a zest for life. The pronouncement is larger than life. Carrying through with it is smaller.

We went to visit her three weeks after she was situated. It was customary for the left-over family to plan for this, it being part of the medical adjustment program for the patient. We even got a classy engraved script invitation/reminder on thick cream paper ("We formally invite you to a last showing of the body . . .")

A plague had fallen on New York City: taxi strike. We needed to get to the airport. Daddy disliked leaving his car in a lot at Kennedy.

I casually mentioned the situation to Nate, not fishing or anything. "You drive us, hear?"

He heard, phoned my father to offer his services as pallbearer, and so it was arranged.

I asked him, "Did your secretary make the call?"

He answered in good form. "Of course not. That would be for business. I dialed direct."

"Well, what is this? Pleasure?"

"No, duty."

"To who?"

"To you."

Feeling sad for someone else is the *duty* of a grownup. What a grim future.

I knew if I ate I'd throw up until the bitter bile came, and I didn't want to taste that. Nate must have been eating secretly, like when I went to the john, because he was always there for me. He let me cry. He made me laugh. He left me alone. But he was always there.

"It would have been better if she'd died, Nate."

"For you or for her?"

"For the way things are. Things are so unreal."

"For your mother they are, Puss. Don't superimpose. For you, 'things,' as you put it, are life. The effect is with you because you can handle it. The horror is with her because she can't."

He seemed to know a lot about dealing with tragedy. Strange, but during those days he was more comfortable with me than ever before. He knew what to do, what to say, how to touch me, the darkness of the room, the right magazines and books, everything. It was as though he'd rehearsed how to be kind.

Daddy had two drinks during the flight. They call them cocktails but they're not. One-hundred-proof anything is what's poured in those little plastic glasses. He didn't look so hot, nobody recognized him. He lit a cigarette before the sign said he could. I undid my seat belt, which was allowed. "Are you relieved?"

He put his head back. "Yes. I think I am."

Our plane would surely crash. "What? No guilt?"

He took a slug of his drink, and then did a hit-the-spot ahhh. "Sounds anti-Semitic, but no guilt. A guilty man is a condemned one."

My private thoughts were screaming "Selfish, selfish!" My public self felt selfless. How good to say once in a while to someone you've done time loving, "Oh, how I hate you." Hate. The emotion so denied and so prevalent. It would be almost kind to let it out in the open so that people don't go crazy with the fear of it.

It was the first time we'd really talked since the phone call. Flying does not bring out the best in people. Perhaps that's due to the universal boarding thought—this is it. Women tend to overdress, equating death to an off season in Miami. Conversation is always at a premium. People rarely snub each other during engine trouble. And everyone devours the ratty little meal, even old people with tubes. Once airborne, there is generally no restraint in dealing with life when it's challenged.

With a decent percentage of alcohol in his blood, I felt Marvin was ready. He started to open the plastic sack containing earphones, to plug himself out.

I took away the toy. "Were there other Lollys?"

He bucked. "What am I under, the truth serum?"

I used my lobster technique. "Were there?"

"I suppose. But not as young."

Leave the claw—into the roe. "How unhappy were you?"

"Very."

Now the cracker. "Why didn't you do something about it?"

"I got used to it."

A dip into the melted butter. "That's worse, isn't it?"

His body twitched as if surfacing from a deep

sleep. "When one feels nothing, it makes one do desperate things." He sucked on a piece of ice.

"Hey, that's what Mummy did, suck ice."

He smiled. His first sensory reaction. "Is it? I guess we weren't married for nothing, then."

"How will you treat her?"

"Preeepare for landing," instructed the fiberglass voice.

Marvin straightened his tie along with his thoughts. "Could you repeat the question?"

• • •

Waiting to disembark, he gave me my answer. "I'll treat her like a child, the way she always wanted me to."

And once more with the crackers. "Is that how you treated Lolly?"

"Yes. But she resented it."

It was a house on a quiet street in a posh suburb of Boston. It was done well, avoiding any obvious hospital signals. Had I not known, I would have thought it a charming place to live. It was expensive, but Daddy could write it off as a tax deduction. It was fitting. He'd written my mother off a long time ago.

We'd decided not to go in her room together. We didn't want her to feel any competition. It was her visit, not ours. Daddy had talked over the phone to her main psychiatrist before we'd left. He'd said that we'd find her no better. He'd implied that it wasn't just a temporary breakdown, but that hers had a lifetime guarantee attached.

Daddy went in first, to get it over with. I didn't blame him. I just felt very sad and very old. And wise, and thankful. You don't dwell on your health that much until someone else is left without it. As I watched him walk down the corridor, I couldn't help mouthing "bastard." The nicest bastard in the world.

I did all of the standard waiting-room things—leafing through magazines, fiddling, extra trips to the bathroom, revving up nerves.

Marvin came out with the same expression that he'd had going in—tolerant. He'd given her ten minutes. Next. My turn for induction. I had planned nothing, except not to cry. I walked straight past him, wanting no contact, and entered the room.

The windows were open, allowing the springtime to come in. There were no flowers. There was nothing. She looked a lot more like a normal sort of mother. Bed jacket, pillows propping her up, no make-up, crow's feet. A mother, a wife. She was in for five days for a hysterectomy, a simply, womanly operation

. . . I wanted to tap my heels together three times to make it true.

"Mummy? It's Prudence."

Wrong. She was irritated. "I know! For God's sake! You came out of me."

I wanted to leave her with her poor muddled mind. I wanted to run out.

The bed had either just been made, or else she hadn't moved at all during the night. Better if she had tossed fitfully. That would have meant she was alive.

"Mummy, I brought you some *Turtle Bay Gazettes* . . ."

"Oh."

God, I wanted my mother. Who was this crazy lady? How did she manage to climb inside?

"Then I arranged to have your subscription sent here . . . so you'll have one every week . . . Mummy? Do you like that idea? You can read it with your morning coffee just like at home."

Her eyes weren't vacant. I was sure that she was receiving. Her hair had so many strands of gray. At least it wasn't white. Hair turned white when people went mad in those terrible ghost stories that children tell.

"Prudence?"

I jumped, startled by her initiative. "What, Mummy?"

"They don't have good coffee here."

We were communicating!

"I'm sorry. Shall I see what I can do about it?"

"Oh . . . oh yes, yes."

She clenched her hand around a piece of sheet.

"Mummy? Can I get you anything?"

She held on tighter. Her knuckles went white. "I want to have a morning."

I couldn't see. I started for the door.

"Prudence?"

I had to get out. I couldn't throw myself on her. "What, Mummy?"

I could feel her strain, like a baby, constipated. "I never was beautiful . . . they just said I was. That doesn't make it so."

I let the tears go, without even closing the door behind me.

Books and screenplays have been dedicated to what happens in airports. People split up, come together, babies are born, people collapse and die. None of life's subtleties. Muzak and chrome.

Marvin and Prudence Goodrich, prominent author and his daughter, boarded a four P.M. plane from Logan Airport to Kennedy. Neither carried any diverting literature. They had approximately one hour of air time together. They needed it.

My father found the obviously attractive stewardess attractive. His theory was that when you went first-class, you deserved something to fly on besides the second-class champagne. Going to Boston he'd been occupied with matters not quite as comely as the Miss Easy Eastern Airlines who was hanging up his coat. Going, he'd still been a man on parole, ordering his drinks straight up and acting melancholy—an attitude quite different from your average widower, who is numb and abstinent—at least until the body is interred. Not the case of Marvin Goodrich. He only needed an acquittal to put him on the comeback trail.

Here was a new man with my father's old clothes on. I talked silently to my old friend, the cashmere sweater, while he ordered champagne—white for him, pink for (the little lady) me.

"Daddy, oh, Daddy—there's still a life up in Boston . . . a *life* . . ."

I already heard the whiskey voices of the cocktail party ladies:

"It must be hormone shots."

"Goat glands."

"Switzerland?"

"Boston—domestic now."

"... looks divoon ... simply ..."

"He had a wife, you know."

"*Finito!* ..."

"... v–e–r–y available ..."

Not to me he wasn't. He wouldn't meet my eyes, which had been weeping for someone he needed to shrug off.

He was suffering from lack of emotion. His voice leaned over. "A little bubbly, baby?"

I would have refused had I not seen the movement of the liquid in the glass he offered. His hand was shaking.

"What are we celebrating?" I asked.

"My relief."

When you love someone, you trust what they say as being their truth. A toast to my Daddy:

"Here's to you as good as you are.
And here's to me as bad as I am.
And as good as you are,
And as bad as I am,
I'm as good as you are
As bad as I am!"

I'd given him a direct quote from the sealed lips of Lolly Spitz to test him on his history. He turned rheumy eyes on me, accepting his hell again for a moment. "Why not just throw me the one about the

Helen Keller doll that you wind up and it runs into the wall?"

His defenses were down. He was trying to get mine up. "I'm not into sick jokes, Daddy."

Whoever was piloting the plane had not had a good breakfast. Burping and weaving, farting and dodging, it couldn't have been keeping on course. I felt queasy and Marvin looked as though he might have used his bag at any second. But we continued.

"You're giving me little chance. We either talk Lolly or Mommy," he said.

I remembered the Lolly estimate of Russians and Poles. "Same difference," I said.

He shrugged his eyebrows, like a Dagwood beset by too many Blondies. "Yeah, I screwed up both of them. I mean, that is your daughterly implication, isn't it? That I screw up my women?"

I wanted to kiss him on both cheeks and call it a flight. "No, you don't." If I let it go it would mean another year tacked onto the doctor's bill. "Yes. You do. But you couldn't keep it up. You had the wrong material to work with."

Then he said a flat, vanilla thing. "Men can't give."

"Nate Spitz can." It popped out from me. That

set both of us on the defensive. At least Mommy and Lolly were common ground.

Despite obvious nausea, he refilled his glass, holding it up, toast position. "Here's to the exception . . . Are you in love with the exception?"

I had frightful sicky stomach, but certain things were expected of me. My back was put straight. My chin lifted. I leveled. "He is a very, very good person."

Marvin laughed sourly. "That's not so hot."

My chin jutted. "He's my dear friend, which can be much more sustaining than the hots, I'll tell ya!"

Marvin put his chair all the way back . . . needed to take things lying down. He wisely left Nate. "So you must have talked with Lolly just before that phone call, the one that all but dismantled me."

I felt somewhat refreshed. Nate didn't belong to the family of breast-beating. "Yes, the day before. But I only heard her side."

His eyes were shut. I closed mine. Two tin cups . . .

"I'll bet she was positive, determined to be dewy."

My eyes were clamped so tightly that I saw white. "How did you know?"

"Because seventeen-year-old girls like Lolly can't and won't be hurt yet."

The no-smoking—fasten-seatbelt sign flashed on.

I clasped his hand . . . couldn't tell which was the icier.

"She was planning on lime-green, being that it was your second marriage."

We were landing. Poorly.

"Oh, my dear God. The only marriage plan I have is *not* to be."

The plane was on the ground, racing past our conversation. Last licks were needed. "So it's kaput for both of them?"

He undid my seatbelt. "I can no longer cope with my marriage and I already have a daughter."

The (no less) prominent author, Marvin Goodrich, and his daughter arrive—Kennedy . . . five-ten P.M.

Parting words to each other as they enter the same taxi:

"Daddy, I love you much."

"It's returned."

"You used to say 'in full.'"

"You used to need it."

"Nate? I'm home."

"I would have come to pick you up! Why didn't you call from the airport?"

"Because."

"Prude, are you all right?"

"Ya. Know why I didn't call from the airport? It's because . . . I forgot your number."

"Oh, is that all? Do you know your last name?"

"Ya. It's Goodrich."

I heard him smile. "Could be. I'll come over to call for you in about twenty minutes. You can take a nap here if you want to."

"Nate?"

"What, Puss?"

"Hi."

"Hi, Puss. I'm glad you're back."

I conked out for about three hours on Nate's bed. Nothing remotely erotic about the sleep of the needy. I had five and a half nightmares, and woke up with terrible breath, a bit let down that Nate wasn't at my bedside awaiting the opening of my lids.

I did some arm stretching and almost knocked my eye out. There was a rock on the fourth finger of my left hand. Talk about your fairy tales. I'd nearly been a Cyclops.

I turned on the light for inspection. That was the one finger whose nail was bitten down to the quick. The ring itself was most presentable. Platinum and a diamond. Conventional. What did I expect, love beads? I was still groggy from sleeping my mother off. In any other circumstance I would have gone racing through rooms in search of my betrothed. Instead I fell back on the bed. The diamond should have made me feel legitimate, proof that I was cared about. It didn't. I felt like a tart whose fiancé had finally come through with the cash. Nate had "done right by me," was going to "make an honest woman of me," "the wife." Morty Manowitz, our accountant, would have gifted me with this ring. Oh, there was a "fuckin' quality difference" to be sure. Morty's would have come from a dealer buddy of his. Nate's ring was probably bought at Cartier's. I took it off and sucked it, hoping that it would melt and in its place would be Nate saying, right on, "Get your ass over here and marry me."

Three weeks ago I'd wished for this. Perhaps not a diamond (jade would have done nicely, jade), but some unveiling of his intentions. Funny. The hardest part of reality comes when you get what you want.

Nate would be in soon. He would be eager to see my reaction to the news on my finger. I think men are pleased with themselves when they give materially, and don't know quite what's come over them when they give emotionally.

I went to the mirror to see the ring in another perspective. Without the harsh light, it had a fragile quality. It looked almost old. Bringing the lamp to the mirror, I watched the reflection to see if it would become a bauble again. No, the ring was not new. I'd almost spoiled something special with my preconceived ideas. I raced, then, through rooms.

He was in the kitchen, preparing a tray for me. Nothing had changed.

"Did you rest your ass, Prude?"

"Yup. It's doing very well, thank you."

"Do you want sick food or well food? I set up a tray and a place at the table. Thought you might be having the vapors in there and just want an egg."

Thank God for the cleaner's bag. He knew what he was doing. Raw emotions are so messy. Understanding them isn't.

"I eat what you eat. But I'll be hungrier if we chat a bit first."

He took off an imaginary apron and cake-walked me into the living room.

"Shall we sit on the settee, Nathan?"

"This frog's not quite up to courtin' tonight, Puss."

He loved me, but he was tired. I still had to learn when to curb being seventeen. I sat on the arm of his chair, rubbing the tender part of his neck, kissing his temple. I tried to keep light. I did try. "The ring was hers, wasn't it?"

Nothing showed. He was breathing easily. "Yes. It was."

"I feel like the second Mrs. De Winter."

It was "rueful" night again. "She's dead, Puss. She's dead enough for the ring to be only yours."

I couldn't help wanting to know. Lolly had said he'd tell me. "Nate . . ."

I needed permission. We were completely quiet. I waited, he prepared. Then he lifted me onto his lap, cupping a breast, rocking me ever so slightly. "Yes. Yes, she did."

I hung onto him as he rocked me. I acknowledged the wink of his pinky ring. Then I had to cry, not for the knowing, but for what I didn't want to know.

I was five years old, with a thirty-carat diamond on the fourth finger of my left hand.

The announcement was mailed out on Friday. "They" should receive it today. "They" will react to it:

Mr. Marvin Goodrich
proudly announces the marriage
of his daughter Prudence
to Mr. Nathan G. Spitz

When I threw my bouquet, Lolly was busy. She was charming someone's male cousin or nephew. He looked young. Our age.

My father was standing alone. He used both hands to catch the flowers.

About the Author

JULIE GOLDSMITH was born in New York City and educated there. She attended Boston University as a drama student and, under the name Julie Gilbert, has acted in stock, repertory, television and films throughout the country. She is Edna Ferber's grandniece, and this inheritance, together with the fact that she was only twenty-four when she wrote *Umbrella Steps,* seems to give promise of a really exciting literary career. Julie Goldsmith Gilbert, actress turned writer, now lives in New York City and is hard at work on her second novel.

The Prophecy

Even the book morphs!
Flip the pages
and check it out!

ANIMORPHS®

titles in Large-Print Editions:

#31 The Conspiracy

#32 The Separation

#33 The Illusion

#34 The Prophecy

#35 The Proposal

#36 The Mutation

ANIMORPHS®

The Prophecy

K.A. Applegate

Gareth Stevens Publishing
A WORLD ALMANAC EDUCATION GROUP COMPANY

For a free color catalog describing Gareth Stevens' list of high-quality books and multimedia programs, call 1-800-542-2595 (USA) or 1-800-461-9120 (Canada). Gareth Stevens Publishing's Fax: (414) 332-3567.

Library of Congress Cataloging-in-Publication Data available upon request from publisher. Fax: (414) 332-3567 for the attention of the Publishing Records Department.

ISBN 0-8368-2757-0

This edition first published in 2000 by
Gareth Stevens Publishing
A World Almanac Education Group Company
330 West Olive Street, Suite 100
Milwaukee, WI 53212 USA

Published by Gareth Stevens, Inc., 330 West Olive Street, Suite 100, Milwaukee, Wisconsin 53212 in large print by arrangement with Scholastic Inc., 555 Broadway, New York, New York 10012.

Cover illustration by David B. Mattingly.
Art direction/design by Karen Hudson.

Printed in the United States of America

1 2 3 4 5 6 7 8 9 04 03 02 01 00

The author wishes to thank Melinda Metz for her assistance in preparing this manuscript.

For Michael and Jake

The Prophecy

CHAPTER 1

My name is Cassie.

Just Cassie. At least that's all I'm going to tell you. It's not because I think I'm so special I only need one name. I know I'm not Jewel or Brandy or Beck.

I'm actually pretty ordinary. If you saw me walking down one of the halls at your school, you probably wouldn't give me a second look. Unless it was one of the days when I had a little bird poop on my jeans from working with my dad in his Wildlife Rehabilitation Clinic. If it was a bird-poop day, you might give me a second "oh-gross" look.

But I really am your basic, average girl. A first and last name plus middle initial kind of girl. Ex-

cept for the fact that I spend most of my time trying to stop the Yeerk invasion of Earth.

That's why I can only tell you my first name. If the Yeerks knew my last name, I'd be dead. No, worse than dead.

Let me give you the Cliffs Notes version.

Fact: Yeerks are alien parasites that have the appearance of small gray slugs. They enter their hosts through the ear canal, then spread their soft bodies into the crevices of their hosts' brains.

Fact: The Yeerks have already enslaved many species, including the Hork-Bajir, the Gedds, and the Taxxons, although the Taxxons submitted willingly. Now the Yeerks have targeted the entire human race for use as hosts.

Fact: You already know someone who is controlled by a Yeerk. You just don't know you know someone who is controlled by a Yeerk. Yeerks can access their hosts' memories and make them act exactly the way they always have. A human host, called a Controller, cannot move a single muscle unless the Yeerk in his or her head gives the order.

Fact: The Animorphs may be your only hope of escaping becoming a human-Controller yourself.

The Animorphs are me and four of my friends — Jake, Rachel, Marco, and Tobias. A great Andalite prince named Elfangor gave us the power to morph into animals. He knew he was about to die, and he didn't want to leave Earth completely defenseless against the Yeerks. Later we were joined in our fight by Elfangor's younger brother, Ax. Aximili-Esgarrouth-Isthill.

Usually the six of us work as a team, but tonight I had a secret mission, and I didn't want too many people around. I asked Rachel if she'd be my backup, and of course she agreed.

You should see Rachel. She's like Stone Cold Steve Austin crossed with Miss Teen USA. Unlike me, Rachel is someone who could pull off the whole I'm-so-special-I-only-need-one-name deal even if she didn't have to keep her identity a secret.

"So are we going in or what?" Rachel asked me.

I stared up at the old Victorian house. A single light burned in one window. A loose shutter kept swinging back and forth on its hinges. The screeching sound made the hair at the back of my neck prickle.

"We're going in," I answered, ignoring the prickling sensation.

"This plan of yours is . . . what's the word I'm looking for?" Rachel asked. "Oh, yeah. Insane. As in Looney Toeowww —"

Rachel's words turned into a high meow. Her vocal cords had started to change first.

"We have to do this," I told her as her nose narrowed and sprouted fur. "It's life and death."

I watched Rachel for a few more moments. She was going to use her cat morph to go into the house. I was going to use my rat morph. I figured it couldn't hurt to give her a little head start. That way she'd be in total control of her cat brain before I became all small and delicious.

When a fluffy black-and-white tail sprang out of Rachel's rear, I decided I'd waited long enough. I focused on the rat DNA inside me, and instantly felt my hands begin to wither.

Morphing is easier for me than anyone else in the group. Maybe it's because I spend so much time around animals. I don't know.

But even for me, morphing isn't a smooth transformation. It's not like my body shrinks first, then grows hair, then shoots out whiskers and a tail.

No, morphing is a lot less logical than that. Grosser, too. Like right now I had little tiny hands, and I could feel coarse hair popping out on my back. But otherwise, I still looked like me.

Then my ears rolled up to the top of my head, and my eyeballs contracted until they were the size of BBs. I felt a sloshing, twisting sensation as my internal organs began to shift and shrink.

My nose and mouth stretched, merged, then re-formed. My teeth sharpened. A wave of dizziness engulfed me as I fell toward the ground, my body shrinking to the size of a . . . of a rat. My hairless, ropey tail appeared and I was done.

<Dog door by the porch, but the dog pee smells in the yard are stale,> Rachel announced in thought-speak.

My little rat heart was racing. My little rat brain was ordering me to run, run, run away from the cat. I clamped down on my new instincts. It's easier when you've already morphed a particular animal before, as I had done with the rat. The first time can be tough, though.

<After you,> I answered.

Rachel took off across the lawn, her body low to the ground. I scurried behind her. The grass brushed up against my belly and tickled my nose.

Without a sound, Rachel slipped through the dog door. <You could have held it open for me,> I complained. I gave the door a head butt. It opened wide enough for me to scramble through.

<There was only one light on,> I reminded Rachel. <Upstairs. Left. Let's try there first.>

We beat feet to the staircase. It would take me forever to haul myself up all those stairs. I decided to take the rat ramp instead. I dug my claws into the wood and climbed the side of the banister. Then I ran straight up.

Of course, Rachel still got to the top before me. I half-climbed, half-fell off the banister and followed her down the hall to the lighted room. I hoped we hadn't gotten here too late.

I took a quick peek inside. Yes! My math teacher was sitting at a desk grading papers. At least I knew this was the right place.

I ducked back. <We have to wait until —>

EEEEEEE!

<She saw us!> Rachel cried. <Get out! Now!>

<That wasn't her,> I shot back. <Teakettle. She'll be coming out. Hide!>

I pressed myself tight against the wall. I squeezed my eyes shut tight so she wouldn't see them glistening in the shadows.

I felt the floor begin to vibrate. Did she see me? Did she see me?

No. Her big feet walked right on by.

<Now's our chance,> Rachel said. <Let's do it!> She darted into the room and leaped up onto the desk. <What am I looking for exactly?>

<A doodle. It's, um, of a . . . a heart,> I stammered. I tried to climb up the desk leg. But it was metal. My claws couldn't get a grip.

<Think I see it,> Rachel answered. <If the heart has "Cassie Loves Jake" printed in the

middle with a really dorky cupid drawn next to it.>

<That's it. I accidentally turned it in with my test. Just get it. And don't say anything,> I warned Rachel.

<Nothing?>

<Nothing! Not. One. Word.>

Rachel laughed and leaped down off the desk with the sheet of paper in her teeth. <Okay, you're my best friend. So not one word. Especially not "Awww, isn't that sweet?" And definitely not "Cassie is in lo-ove, Cassie is in lo-ove." And no way I'd ever say —>

<I knew I should have done this alone.>

CHAPTER 2

The cool night air fluttered my owl feathers as I flapped toward home. I tightened my right talon around the doodle. There was no way I was going to lose it again.

I still couldn't believe I'd turned it in to a teacher. Was love turning my brain to mush, or what? I wondered if Jake ever did stupid stuff because he was daydreaming about me.

We never talked about things like that. We'd never even used the "L" word to each other. That's what Rachel calls it. The "L" word.

But even though he'd never said it out loud, I knew that Jake loved me. And I knew Jake knew I loved him, even though I'd never said it out loud, either.

That was totally clear when we kissed. Yes, even though we don't walk around groping each other like some couples, we have kissed a few times. Usually right after we've managed to survive something horrible. It's usually an "I-can't-believe-we're-alive!" kiss.

Not that I'm complaining. Well, not exactly. I have to admit it would be nice to kiss Jake after a movie instead of after a battle or some other near-death experience.

I dropped one wing and made a sharp turn. The back of our barn came into sight.

Hork-Bajir!

The distinctive nightmare shape moved through the shadows that were bright as day to me. Just one. One was enough.

Shouldn't be here! Couldn't be here! The Yeerks, they had to know everything!

No!

The image of my parents being ripped to bits by the Hork-Bajir's blades blasted into my brain. Images of other Yeerks rounding up my friends. Doors kicked in, Dracon beams firing, flashing blades. Rachel. Jake.

No! NO!

Couldn't worry about them. Not now. Focus! Had to stop this one Hork-Bajir. Just this one. Then . . .

Land on the other side of the barn, demorph, then morph to wolf, attack, attack!

No time. It would take too long. Too late! The Hork-Bajir could . . . what was a lone Hork-Bajir doing here? One by himself? Irrelevant! Focus!

What would Rachel do? Attack right now. She wouldn't wait to morph. She'd swoop down and rake the Hork-Bajir with her talons.

Attack now.

I focused on the Hork-Bajir and flew straight for it. I'd aim for the eyes. While it was staggering around blind, I'd morph from owl to human to wolf. Or polar bear. Then I'd go for the throat. I could almost taste the flesh already.

Closer. Closer. I stretched out my talons, preparing to strike. A noiseless night-stalker designed by nature for much smaller prey.

I flew between the light above the shed and the Hork-Bajir. The Hork-Bajir spun, alerted by my shadow. He would slice me in half!

Then, in the light, at the last possible moment . . .

<Aaaahhh!>

I jerked my talons back and spun my body hard to the left. I crash-landed in the dirt a few feet away from the Hork-Bajir. I wasn't hurt but I was definitely shaking.

I lay there on my side in the dirt, a wing crumpled beneath me. <Hi, Jara Hamee,> I said. <Lovely night for a walk.>

This Hork-Bajir wasn't a Controller, wasn't a creature of the Yeerks. It was Jara Hamee, one of the tiny group of free Hork-Bajir. I'd almost blinded him. The thought made me nauseous.

But my entire universe was being put back in place in my mind now. No attack on my parents. The Yeerks did not know about us. No violent assault to seize Jake and Rachel, Ax and Tobias and Marco.

None of that was happening. And eventually my heart would stop hammering like it was trying to get out of my rib cage.

I concentrated on my own DNA and demorphed as fast as I could. <What are you doing here, Jara? It's too dangerous for you to be away from your valley.>

The colony of free Hork-Bajir lives in a hidden valley created for them by a being called the Ellimist. Even if you know exactly where it is, it's hard to find. Your eyes just seem to slide away from it. Your mind just seems to want to forget it. It's the only place that the Hork-Bajir are at all safe from the Yeerks. Or from humans for that matter. Most humans who saw a Hork-Bajir would shoot first, ask questions later. It's not hard to understand why. The Hork-Bajir look as if they were designed to kill. But they are among the gentlest creatures I've ever encountered.

They're even vegetarians. The razor-sharp blades on their ankles, knees, wrists, and elbows are for stripping bark off trees. That's what they eat. Bark.

"Need help," Jara answered. "Toby say, 'Father, get human friends. Bring.'"

I emerged into fully human form. "Why? What happened? What's wrong?" I demanded. Amazing how now my human heart was still beating way too fast from the adrenaline rush of sheer terror.

Jara rocked back and forth on his big T. Rex feet. "Alien come valley."

"The Yeerks? They found you?!" I cried. "Did they attack you? What's the situation?"

Talking to Jara Hamee was sort of like talking to a four-year-old. Which was fine usually. But not now. Every second wasted could be putting the free Hork-Bajir in danger.

"Not Yeerks," Jara explained. "Arn. From the old world. Arn . . . make . . . Hork-Bajir."

CHAPTER 3

<An Arn, on Earth? Here? Why? That's the question. What's he up to?> Rachel wondered.

<He had to come. *Star Wars: The Phantom Menace* isn't coming out on DVD there for, like, two years. He buys up a bunch of copies here, takes 'em home, makes a fortune.>

<Good grief, Marco, you live science fiction, why do you want to *watch* science fiction?>

<Don't be dissing TPM,> Marco said. <Cool is cool.>

The whole group was in bird-of-prey morph. It was the fastest way to get to the Hork-Bajir valley. The night had passed. The sun had come up on a new day. A beautiful, cool Saturday morn-

ing. The deep green forest foothills below us, the towering cumulus above. It was almost hot in the direct sunlight, cooler under the shadow of the Mount Everest-sized clouds.

<If he's hoping to pick up some new slaves in the colony, he can forget it,> Rachel continued. <The Hork-Bajir are never going to be Arn slaves again. We'll see to that.>

Rachel wasn't being totally accurate. The Hork-Bajir were never slaves on their home planet. Not exactly. It's not like the Arn made the Hork-Bajir wait on them hand and foot.

What we knew of all this came from Tobias, who'd heard the story from Jara Hamee. There was a terrible cataclysm on the planet we call the Hork-Bajir home world, but in those days the planet was populated only by the Arn. It shattered the planet's crust and stripped away much of the atmosphere. The Arn who survived needed trees to provide oxygen. Lots of exceedingly large trees. They didn't feel like taking care of the trees themselves. Solution? They used genetic engineering to design creatures of low intelligence who ate tree bark: the Hork-Bajir.

An elegantly simple solution for the Arn who were masters of genetic manipulation.

The Hork-Bajir just lived their lives, utterly unaware that the Arn even existed deep down in the impossibly steep valleys. They took care of the trees they depended on for food. They did what came naturally. Did what the Arn designed them to do.

Then came the Yeerks.

The Yeerks didn't see tree maintenance workers when they saw the Hork-Bajir. They saw an army. They made the Hork-Bajir their hosts. They took the peaceful creatures away from their home planet and began using them as killing machines, shock troops of the Yeerk Empire.

There's a longer story there, but that's the short version.

<Rachel, you know, there are some nice thermals today, we have a sweet little tailwind,> Tobias said. <You don't have to exhaust yourself with all that flapping.>

Tobias is the expert. Tobias is, or was, trapped in red-tailed hawk morph. He regained his ability to morph, but he's chosen to consider hawk as his true body.

Long story there, too.

I stretched open my wings and caught one of those thermals. The warm air lifted up my osprey body.

A couple of thermals later I spotted about twenty Hork-Bajir clustered together in the center of the valley. Adults and kids. Seeing the kids was especially cool. They were the first Hork-Bajir in generations to be born into freedom.

We circled down from the clouds and landed, one by one. All of us demorphed, except Tobias.

Toby Hamee moved away from the group to greet us. Toby is the daughter of Jara Hamee and Ket Halpak. She's what the Hork-Bajir call "different." She's what the Arn call a freak of nature. She is a seer. A Hork-Bajir whose intelligence matches that of the Arn themselves.

"Thank you for coming. We felt the need of your advice."

"No problemo," Marco said. "It was either this or wash my dad's car."

"The Arn landed last evening in a small Yeerk ship. We nearly killed him, thinking he was a Controller. He has some sort of plan in mind. We told him to wait so we could bring you to advise us."

"We're flattered," Jake said, "but you don't need us."

"I do need you," Toby said. "I especially need you," she added, looking at Ax. "If I understand his goal, we could use an Andalite's opinion."

"Let's see what he's got to say," Jake said.

We followed Toby over to the Hork-Bajir. They moved closer together to make room for us in the circle.

The Arn stood in the center. The first thing I noticed about him was his eyes. They glittered like diamonds lit from within. Their intensity dazzled me.

I blinked a few times, and began to take in more details of the Arn's appearance. He had four legs, two elongated arms, and a pair of short wings. He was about half as tall as Ax and his skin was a vibrant emerald-green.

I stared at the Arn. We'd gotten almost used to seeing alien races: Hork-Bajir, Taxxons, Andalites, Howlers. Almost. There was still something unsettling about seeing something, someone who was so definitely not from around here.

And even by the standards of aliens, the Arn was bizarre. He stood, surrounded by seven-foot-tall nightmares, watched by a deceptively peaceful-looking Andalite, a hawk, and a gaggle of badly dressed kids.

And he was still the strangest being there. And all the more strange to me because I could see, or felt I could see, a deep, unreachable sadness behind those glittering, unhuman eyes.

"These are humans," the Arn said, nodding. "Yes. I spent a day waiting in orbit, learning your languages. You have many interesting languages but your biology is not at all remarkable, I'm afraid. Two arms, two legs, a most unstable platform. And entirely lacking in physical innovation: simple bilateral symmetry for the most part."

"Yeah, nice to meet you, too," Rachel said. "What are you up to, what do you want?"

"I am Arn."

<We know about the Arn,> Tobias said. <We know your species.>

If the glittery-eyed creature was shocked at being addressed by a bird he didn't show it.

"I am Quafijinivon," he said. "The species you claim to know is no more. And I am the last of the Arn.

CHAPTER 4

"I have come to give the Hork-Bajir a chance for freedom and rebirth. And revenge against the Yeerks. I have a plan that will require your assistance."

"Who's going to give them a shot at revenge against you, Arn?" Rachel muttered.

"Ten bucks says whatever he has in mind ends up with us screaming and running," Marco said.

Quafijinivon's small red mouth pursed disapprovingly. "I have very little time, humans. No time at all for pleasantries. I will live for only four hundred and twelve more days, give or take a few hours, that is a biological fact."

<There are forces other than biology,> Ax

said. He gave his deadly tail just the slightest little twitch.

"Yes, well, an Andalite. Charming, as always." He made a grimace that might have been a smile. "Recently I intercepted a Yeerk transmission and learned to my amazement that a free Hork-Bajir colony existed on Earth. I risked everything to steal a Yeerk ship, and have traveled a great distance to find —"

"Do the Yeerks know the location of the colony?" Jake interrupted.

"No," Quafijinivon answered. "I found it myself. We Arn long ago developed technology to track our —"

"What exactly is this plan of yours?" Rachel demanded.

The Arn shot her a quelling look, clearly displeased to have been interrupted a second time. "My plan is to collect samples of the DNA of the free Hork-Bajir. With their permission," he added quickly. "I would then use the DNA to create a new colony on my home planet."

<To do what? Fight the Yeerks for you?> Tobias asked. He edged back and forth on the log he was using as a perch. <Is that what you meant when you said the Hork-Bajir would get revenge?>

I could practically feel the disapproval coming off him. Tobias is probably closer to the Hork-

Bajir than any of the rest of us. Toby Hamee is named after him. Toby for Tobias.

"To fight the Yeerks, yes," Quafijinivon replied. "But not for me. To regain their planet. To regain what the Yeerks took from them."

And from you, I thought. I'm usually pretty good at figuring out people's motives. But I wasn't sure what the Arn's deal was yet. Was he trying to help the Hork-Bajir? Or was he just trying somehow to help himself?

Jake shook his head. "Even if the Hork-Bajir agreed, how would some small colony win a war against the Yeerks? No ships. No orbital weapons platforms. Not even handheld Dracon beams."

"Yeah, the Yeerks have these cute little things called weapons," Marco added.

"So would the Hork-Bajir," Quafijinivon answered. "Before they lost their lives to the Yeerks, Aldrea-Iskillion-Falan and Dak Hamee stole an entire transport ship filled with handheld Dracon beams, as well as a good supply of very sophisticated explosives."

I saw Jake and Marco exchange a look.

Marco shrugged. "No question that opening a new front against the Yeerks would be helpful. A guerilla war on the Hork-Bajir home world would pull Yeerk resources away from Earth, away from the Andalites."

"This isn't our fight," I pointed out. I nodded

toward Jara Hamee and Toby. “I think we’re just here to advise.”

Jake winced, realizing he’d been playing boss.

“I will do whatever I can to continue the work of Aldrea and Dak Hamee,” Toby said guardedly. “A DNA sample is little enough to ask.”

Aldrea and Dak were Toby’s great-grandparents. They were heroes to the Hork-Bajir because they had led the battle against the Yeerks. And lost their lives in the fight.

“I give, too,” Jara answered.

The other Hork-Bajir all chimed in. All agreeing to allow Quafijinivon to harvest their DNA, despite the fact that none of them besides Toby had any idea what DNA was.

Quafijinivon lowered his head. “I thank you,” he told them. “But that is only the beginning. There is one more thing I must ask before I can move forward with my plan.”

“Uh-oh,” Marco said in a loud stage whisper. “Here it comes.”

The Arn turned his weird eyes toward me and the other Animorphs. “Aldrea and Dak Hamee hid the weapons. I have been unable to recover them. We Arn are perhaps unequaled in our biological science. But we have no great technological skill.”

<So what do you propose?> Ax asked. <Do you plan to create new Hork-Bajir and send them out to search for the weapons?>

"No. That would be self-defeating. I have something rather more . . . unusual in mind."

<Unusual is our middle name,> Tobias said dryly.

"I have in my possession the *Ixcila* of Aldrea-Iskillion-Falan."

<Seerow's daughter?> Ax exclaimed.

"Ixcila?" Jake repeated.

"Her stored persona," Quafijinivon explained impatiently. "Her brain wave patterns. Her memories. Her personality. Her essence."

His voice had started to sound quavery, and for the first time I realized that he was old and weak. It's impossible to tell the age of an alien till you know what to look for.

"The *Atafalxical* must be performed. It is the only way to unlock the *Ixcila.* But the Ceremony of Rebirth will not succeed unless there is a strong receptacle mind available, a mind as strong as Aldrea's own."

Receptacle mind. The phrase repeated itself in my head until it became nothing more than a jumble of sounds. An echo that felt important but whose meaning I could not grasp.

I felt that something-crawling-up-your-neck sensation that warns of disaster approaching. The tornado is coming, Auntie Em.

"If all goes well, the *Ixcila* will move into the receptacle mind, and we will be able to com-

municate with Aldrea," Quafijinivon continued. "She will be able to lead us to the weapons."

"And what happens to the receptacle?" Jake asked.

"Oh, it will be undamaged, if that is what concerns you," Quafijinivon answered. "The receptacle mind simply shares space with the *Ixcila* until the *Ixcila* is returned to storage."

The Arn pulled in a wheezing breath. "Only one in four Ceremonies are actually completed. The appropriate receptacle mind is essential. Aldrea's *Ixcila* will be attracted to someone most like she was. Someone strong, fierce, independent. Presumably female. Hork-Bajir or Andalite, most likely, but I suppose she might gravitate toward a human. If such a human female existed."

"Oh, I think I know where one could be found," Marco said.

CHAPTER 5

"And the next words out of Rachel's mouth will be . . ."

"I'll do it," Rachel said, giving Marco a self-mocking look.

"Bingo," Marco said.

"I don't consider myself worthy of the honor," Toby said, "but I, too, will volunteer."

I kept quiet. The description fit Rachel and Toby. Not me.

We debated. We argued. Rachel for. Tobias for. Ax and Marco against. Jake listening, weighing, considering whether to once more put us all in harm's way. Me? I just felt unsettled.

I knew how the debate would end. It was a

chance to hurt the Yeerks. It was a chance to help the free Hork-Bajir. A no-brainer, morally or strategically.

Except for the fact that, as Marco pointed out, it was insane. We very seldom ended up refusing to do what was insane.

Quafijinivon asked if there was some more confined space nearby. The Hork-Bajir led us to a cave.

I shivered. I told myself it was because the cave was cold.

<I would like to ask a question,> Ax said. He turned all four of his eyes toward the Arn. <You claim that the receptacle will share space with the *Ixcila* of Aldrea until it is time for it to be returned to storage.>

"That is correct," Quafijinivon answered. His eyes were as bright as stars in the darkness.

<What if Aldrea does not wish to leave the receptacle after she helps us find the weapons?> Ax asked. <Is there some way to force her to do so?>

There was a long moment of silence. The kind of silence that feels as if it sucks half the oxygen out of the air.

"Aldrea must choose to release her hold on the receptacle," Quafijinivon said, not exactly answering the question Ax had asked.

Ax rolled one eye stalk toward Rachel and one

toward Toby. We'd all agreed that Aldrea would be drawn to one of them . . . if the so-called Ceremony worked at all.

Rachel, because of her Rachelness. Toby, because she was Aldrea's great-granddaughter and a Hork-Bajir seer.

<And if she doesn't choose to release her hold?> Ax prodded.

"We could probably sell the story rights to Lifetime for big bucks," Marco commented. "This is so television for women. Two strong, independent girls. One body."

Toby turned to Ax. "You only ask this because you don't trust Aldrea. As an Andalite you mistrust anyone who would choose to permanently become Hork-Bajir," she accused.

Toby's gifts didn't just make her more articulate than the other Hork-Bajir. They made her more insightful. More capable of drawing conclusions.

I wondered if she was right about Ax. The thought of an Andalite choosing to become Hork-Bajir had to be repellent to Ax. Almost sacrilegious. Andalites are not known for their humility.

But I understood Aldrea's choice. More than that, I admired it. I admired her. Aldrea discovered that her own fellow Andalites had created a virus targeted to kill the Hork-Bajir. It was a cold-blooded, military-minded decision. The An-

dalites knew they would lose the Hork-Bajir planet. They knew that if the Hork-Bajir survived in large numbers they would be used as weapons for the Yeerks. And that with such troops the Yeerks would have a much-strengthened chance of conquering other planets throughout the galaxies.

The leader of the desperate Andalite forces on the planet made the call. Later it was disavowed by the Andalite people. Too late to stop what happened. Sometimes, in war, even the "good guys" do awful things.

Once Aldrea learned of the virus, she was forced to choose between her own people and Dak Hamee, the Hork-Bajir seer she had come to love. She chose Dak. She stayed in Hork-Bajir morph until the change became permanent. Aldrea and Dak vowed to fight both the Yeerks and the Andalites. They died keeping this vow.

Ax shifted his weight from one hoof to the other. <I ask only because it is a logical question,> he finally said.

"I did not mean to sound suspicious of my Andalite friend," Toby said with no sincerity whatsoever.

<The Hork-Bajir have reason to be . . . hesitant . . . about trusting the Andalites,> Ax allowed.

Toby bowed her head graciously. Then she said, "I, too, want an answer, Arn."

Quafijinivon sighed. "If Aldrea does not choose to release her hold, there is no way to force her to do so," he confessed.

"I see. I trust my great-grandmother," Toby said firmly. "If she chooses me for this honor I will trust my freedom to her."

"Okay. Rachel? It's your call," Jake told her.

He clearly felt obligated to ask the question even though anyone who knows Rachel also knew what her answer would be.

"I still say let's do it," she said.

No surprise there. Rachel wouldn't have been Rachel if she'd said anything else.

Quafijinivon nodded. He reached into a small metallic pouch hanging from a cord around his neck and pulled out a small vial. The liquid inside glowed green.

"Isn't that what nuclear waste looks like?" Marco asked in a loud whisper.

"We gather to conduct the *Atafalxical,*" Quafijinivon began. "The Ceremony of Rebirth is an occasion for both solemnity and joy, for grieving and celebration."

"Not to mention a severe case of the willies," Marco said under his breath.

If he was close enough I would have elbowed

him. Not that it would have shut him up. Solemnity just isn't part of Marco's repertoire.

Quafijinivon continued with the ceremony as if he hadn't heard Marco. He pulled the stopper out of the vial and a wisp of vapor escaped. A moment later the inside of my nose started to burn, although I couldn't smell anything except the odor of damp cave.

"We call on Aldrea-Iskillion-Falan," Quafijinivon said. He reached into the pouch again. I squinted, trying to see what he'd removed. It looked like a small piece of metal.

It must have been some kind of catalyst, because the instant he dropped it into the vial, the liquid turned from green to a fluorescent scarlet. Its light washed over those closest to it.

Rachel's fair skin appeared to have been drenched in blood. Toby's green flesh had darkened until it was almost black.

Quafijinivon added another piece of metal to the vial. "We call on Aldrea-Iskillion-Falan," he repeated.

"Paging Stephen King," Marco said quietly. "R.L. Stine calling Stephen King with a message from Anne Rice."

The liquid in the vial thickened. It began to contract and expand.

In and out.

In and out.

My heart began to beat to the same rhythm. I could feel it in my chest and in the base of my throat. I could feel it in my ears and in my fingertips.

"We call on Aldrea-Iskillion-Falan. We call on Aldrea-Iskillion-Falan."

Quafijinivon repeated the words again and again, stamping his feet as he cried them out.

"We call on Aldrea-Iskillion-Falan." His voice grew louder. His feet stamped so hard they sent a vibration through the rock floor of the cave.

The liquid in the vial contracted and expanded faster. In and out. In and out. In and out.

My heartbeat matched the new rhythm.

"We. Call. On. Aldrea. Iskillion. Falan," Quafijinivon wailed.

"If I see one single zombie I am —"

The cave floor jerked under my feet. I stumbled forward and landed on my knees in front of the Arn.

"The receptacle has been chosen!" Quafijinivon shouted.

He reached out and put his hand on my head. "Will you accept the *Ixcila* of Aldrea-Iskillion-Falan?"

What? What? She chose me?

That couldn't be right.

"Will you accept the *Ixcila*?" Quafijinivon repeated, his voice echoing in the cave.

"No!" Jake snapped.

But there was only one answer I could give.

"Yes."

CHAPTER 6

I braced myself for . . . for what, I didn't know.

I once had a Yeerk in my head. I know the sensation of another being invading me. I know the violation of having my most private memories exposed. I know the horror of losing control over my own arms and legs and mouth. But I felt none of these things now.

"She chose Cassie?" I heard Rachel mumble. "I feel so ten minutes ago."

"May I speak to my great-grandmother now?" Toby asked eagerly. Her voice was filled with awe. She revealed none of Rachel's bemused resentment.

I swallowed, then swallowed again. My throat

felt as dry and scratchy as sandpaper. "I'm sorry, Toby. I don't think the Ceremony was —" I began. Then I realized something was different.

Have you ever been taking a test and totally blanked? You read a question. You know you know the answer. You know you memorized it when you were studying. But you can't get to it. It's like there's a wall in your brain separating you from the information.

That's how I felt now. And the wall was enormous. High and long and solid.

I was pretty sure Aldrea was on the other side of the wall. But nothing was getting through. I wasn't picking up even a fragment of a thought or a hint of an emotion. The only thing I knew was that something, some force, some bundle of sensations, some object or person was sitting inside my mind.

It was as if she was behind me, or beside me, but turning my head I couldn't see her. There but not visible. There nevertheless.

"Cassie, are you okay? What happened?" Jake asked calmly. Too calmly.

"Did the *Ixcila* take root?" Quafijinivon asked, his voice breaking. It was the first real emotion the Arn had shown. He wanted this to work. Needed it to work.

"Shhh," I said. "Please, just shhh, all of you."

I squeezed my eyes shut. I didn't want any outside stimulus right now.

"Aldrea?" I called aloud, softly, tentatively, feeling like an idiot talking to the dripping, dank cave walls.

No answer.

Aldrea! I repeated, this time silently, hoping she could hear my directed thought. *If you're there, please try to say something to me.*

No answer.

<Well, this is odd,> Tobias said. <Like a séance. All we need is a Ouija board.>

She had to be totally disoriented. I wondered if she'd been able to experience anything while she was in storage. Did she have any idea she had been taken to a planet in a different galaxy? Had she been aware that the Ceremony was taking place? Did she realize she wasn't in the vial now?

Did she know she was dead?

"Aldrea, if you can hear me, I want you to know that you're safe," I said.

"Safe as a dead person can be," Marco said.

<Who's safer than a dead person?> Tobias asked rhetorically.

"Aldrea, you're sharing my brain and body. My name is Cassie. I'm a human girl. I live on planet Earth. An Arn just performed the *Atafal* —"

<Arn?!>

Red dots exploded in front of my eyes. The question in my head was so loud and forceful it made me dizzy.

There was definitely a hole in the wall now. I could feel Aldrea's emotions coming through. Anger was the strongest.

<Where . . . what has . . . what have you done to me, Arn?> she demanded. <What have you done?>

Her voice was a noise like a chainsaw in my brain. "Ah! Ah! Ah! Aldrea, stop! Please, stop! You're hurting me!" I yelled.

Jake grabbed me around the shoulders and held me up. My knees had given way.

I felt a welling up of pain from Aldrea, an echo, and knew that my silent scream had hurt her back.

I pulled in a shaky breath.

"Did you guys hear that? Did she speak through my mouth?" I asked, confused.

"No, we just heard you," Rachel said. "At least, I guess it was you."

Bringing up the Arn was definitely not the way to win Aldrea's trust. I needed another way to reach her. Something that would get through her anger.

"Aldrea, don't say anything for a moment. Just listen. Let me explain," I said softly. When I felt her acceptance, I rushed on. "You were brought to this planet because there is a colony of free Hork-Bajir here. Your grandson, Jara Hamee, is part of the colony. So is your great-granddaughter, Toby Hamee."

I paused to receive Aldrea's reaction. I felt a swirl of too many emotions to take in. I caught traces of curiosity and disbelief, of hope, and fear, and panic. "Toby Hamee is in the cave with us," I continued. "Can you see her? You should be able to see through my eyes."

<All I see is blackness,> she answered.

I glanced around the cave. I wanted something basic to look at. I focused on Rachel's red shirt.

"Maybe you just aren't used to the way my brain gets information from my eyes," I told Aldrea. "Right now, I'm looking at something red."

I felt her concentrating. Then I felt the relief of recognition.

<Red!> Aldrea exclaimed.

I turned toward Toby. <Now I am looking at — is that her? Is that my great-granddaughter?> she interrupted.

"Yes," I answered.

I felt a strange desire to go and press my forehead against Toby's. It took me a moment to realize the desire was Aldrea's.

If Aldrea wanted to touch Toby, why shouldn't she? I started to take a step forward, but a group of rapid-fire questions from Aldrea stopped me.

<I don't understand. What year is this? Where is Dak? How did I get here? What happened to my own body?>

Her panic grew so intense that I felt sweat break out on my forehead.

"I think maybe it's time to call the Exorcist," Marco said. Not a joke, really. He was worried. Everyone was worried.

"Do you remember an old Arn storing your *Ixcila*?" I asked.

<Yes,> she replied. <I agreed to have my persona harvested, although I didn't think the Arn were really advanced enough to make a successful transplant.>

I knew the moment the knowledge hit her. Really hit her. My heart started to pound, and I felt like my nerve endings were getting jolts of electricity.

<But that is what has happened, isn't it? A successful transplant?> Aldrea continued. <This can only mean that —>

I hesitated. But she had to know the truth. "Yes, Aldrea, you are dead."

CHAPTER 7

ALDREA

My name is Aldrea-Iskillion-Falan.

And I have been told that I am dead.

Impossible.

Ridiculous.

The thought patterns the Arn had stored would only allow for a crude reproduction of me. A jumble of facts and sensations. Nothing more. There was no possibility that the thoughts and emotions I was experiencing now could be coming out of electrical impulses and chemicals collected years ago. I must have been knocked unconscious in a battle. A hallucination. A ploy the Yeerks were using to break me. They must be hoping that I —

But what about the body? What about the

hands with too few fingers to be Andalite, the arms too weak and frail to be Hork-Bajir?

I didn't want to believe I was dead. But I could not deny the fact that I was in a body that was not my own. A small, weak, defenseless body covered in furless brown skin.

"Aldrea?" the creature called Cassie said. "Are you all right?"

I realized that I wasn't just hearing her words. I was feeling bits of emotion, too. Empathy and concern and sadness. A little fear, too. Fear for herself.

<Is Dak alive?> I asked, speaking in what felt like my own native tongue of thought-speak. I had to know. Unless . . . no, either way I had to know. The emotions from Cassie gave me my answer before her words.

"No, Aldrea. He died a long time ago. A long way from here. I'm sorry," she answered.

<Where is his *Ixcila*?> I demanded. I knew he had one, too. It could be put into another body the way mine had. Dak and I could still be together.

"I don't know," she answered.

Cassie turned her gaze toward the Arn. It took me a moment to realize that she wasn't communicating with him in the way we had been communicating. It took me a few moments more to comprehend how her brain received input from her ears and how I could use her brain to translate the data into words I could understand.

"The Yeerks did extensive blasting to create level places for training grounds. My lab was heavily damaged. The *Ixcila* of Dak Hamee was destroyed," the Arn explained.

Was it true? If so, then Dak was truly dead. Dead like my parents. Like my brother, Barafin.

<Then let me die, Arn,> I said. <Let me die, too.>

Had I had the chance to say good-bye to Dak? Had we fought side by side until the end? I would never know. My *Ixcila* had been collected before my death, so the memories of my last moments with Dak did not exist.

I felt a wave of sadness from Cassie. I shoved it away. I had no use for her emotions. She was nothing to me.

There was one final question I had to ask, although I was terrified to hear the answer. <My son. What happened to the son I named after my father, Seerow?>

I waited for Cassie to repeat my question.

It was the young Hork-Bajir who answered. "They took him, Great-grandmother. Seerow became a Controller. He was brought to Earth as part of their army, here. He died in captivity."

There was not a worse fate I could have imagined for my child. The Yeerks had made his life a

living death. And I had not been there to protect him.

"But Seerow's son, Jara Hamee, my father, escaped with the help of the humans here," Toby continued. "And I, your great-granddaughter, was born in freedom."

I studied her through my new eyes. There was something about her. Something familiar. The words were too well organized, the speech flowed too smoothly, the ideas . . .

Through my despair I felt a tiny bubble of something that could have been joy.

<Ask her if she's different,> I told Cassie.

A smile spread across Toby's face when she heard the question.

"Yes, Great-grandmother, I am different," she answered. "I am different as Dak Hamee was different."

A seer. A seer born in freedom.

"We have brought you back from death because we need your help," Toby said.

<Tell her that there is nothing she could ask of me that I would not give,> I said to Cassie.

My rebirth had brought me a pain that felt almost unbearable. My Dak gone. My Seerow gone.

But it had brought me a gift as well. The chance to know my great-granddaughter.

I wouldn't give that up for anything. Perhaps I would even see Toby's child one day.

CHAPTER 8

The Arn quickly outlined his plan for Aldrea. I could feel her mistrust and anger growing as he spoke.

"Can you help us?" the Arn asked. "Do you remember where the weapons are hidden?"

<No. I know nothing of any weapons. It must have occurred . . . if it did occur, after,> Aldrea said.

I repeated her message.

The Arn nodded his head sadly. "And yet, it was the mind that found the hiding place. Found once, it could find again. Could Aldrea find them?"

<Could I find weapons I hid? Yes, most likely,> Aldrea said.

"Then the two of us — no, I suppose that should be the three of us, counting the receptacle — will leave tomorrow," Quafijinivon replied. "While the new Hork-Bajir are being grown in my laboratory, you will have time to retrieve the weapons."

"If Cassie goes, we go," Jake said.

"But she is just a vessel," Quafijinivon said with a sort of greasy smile. "Why would you humans need to come?"

<Because you think she's nothing but a vessel, that's why,> Tobias said.

"I hadn't thought to bring —" Quafijinivon began.

<Tell him to be silent,> Aldrea ordered. <This discussion is pointless. I could no doubt find these weapons, but I will not help the Arn —>

<Wait, wait. You're going too fast,> I told her. I found I could communicate mind to mind with her now. As easy as any internal dialogue.

<Then let me use your speech centers. I will speak to them directly.>

A perfectly logical request. I had no real reason for refusing, did I? <If you can access my speech centers, I guess go ahead.>

Almost immediately I felt a tickling sensation in my throat. My tongue gave a twitch and I let out something that sounded way too much like a pig grunting.

"Cassie, you okay?" Rachel asked.

I couldn't answer her. Aldrea had my teeth locked together. I held up both hands and nodded, trying to show everyone that I was okay. My hands were still mine, at least.

"Thh — Thh —"

I could feel little specks of spit flicking down onto my chin. I expected to get at least a "say it, don't spray it" out of Marco, but he stayed quiet.

"Thh. Ihh. This. This. This is Althrea. Drr. Drr. Aldrea. Cass-ie is al-low-ing me to u-se h-er voice," Aldrea explained.

She reminded me of a little kid sounding out words in a book that was too hard for her. She also reminded me of a Yeerk. She was using my mouth! Speaking with my voice!

"I sa-id I wou-ld do an-y-thing to he-l-p my great-gr-and-dau-gh-ter and the Ho-r-k-Ba-ji-r," she continued. "But I wi-ll not do this."

"What do you mean?" the Arn demanded. "You must! You are refusing the chance to give the Hork-Bajirs' planet back to them?" His voice was quivering. I wasn't sure if it was because he was furious or simply exhausted.

Aldrea laughed. It was a harsh, ugly sound that hurt my throat. "No, Arn. I am refu-sing the chance to give you your planet back. That is what you are tru-ly asking. You care no-thing for the Hork-Bajir. Your kind never did."

Her words were coming much more smoothly now. Aldrea was getting comfortable with operating my mouth. I wasn't getting comfortable with letting her. I felt like the world's largest ventriloquist's dummy.

"Ridiculous," the Arn protested. "I am old. Soon I will be dead."

"You're asking me to help you use the Hork-Bajir again. Every time one of your new Hork-Bajir kills a Yeerk he will also be killing one of his own kind." Aldrea asked, "You brought me back to help Hork-Bajir kill Hork-Bajir?"

"What you say is true, Great-grandmother," Toby said. "But there is no other way. Few of our people survived the Andalite virus. Only those who had already been taken off-world by the Yeerks, and those few with natural immunity like you and my great-grandfather. We could grow again, take back our world. But not until we weaken the Yeerks."

Toby stepped up in front of me and leaned down so she could look into my eyes. No. Into Aldrea's eyes, because I might just as well not have been there. "Let me accompany you to our planet. We can start again, continue the work you and Dak Hamee began," Toby pleaded.

I felt another stab of grief from Aldrea when Toby said Dak's name. Then I felt her push that grief aside.

"You are a seer, Toby, but you are also young. You don't know what this Arn, this Andalite, and even, I suspect, these humans, intend. Even well armed, do you think the few Hork-Bajir that this creature, this Arn, this manipulator, this liar from a race of liars, this coward from a race of cowards . . ." She stabbed my finger toward the Arn. I felt my face twist into an expression of fury.

She regained control over her emotions, but now adrenaline was flooding my system. She had triggered the classic human physiological response to stress. And with that hormone rush my own fear and anger grew.

"Hork-Bajir kill Hork-Bajir and who will profit?" Aldrea demanded.

"All the enemies of the Yeerks will profit," Jake said. Toby nodded and said, "True, Great-grandmother, it would be a sideshow. It would only be a distraction for the Yeerks. Many Hork-Bajir would die. And yet we must fight."

Aldrea spread my hands wide. "Why?"

"Because we must be a free people, Great-grandmother. So far our freedom here, in this valley, on this planet, has been bought and paid for by these humans, our friends. But freedom can't be given. It must be taken and held and defended. Our freedom has to be our own creation."

I felt again some measure of Aldrea's sad-

ness. Every word from Toby's mouth reminded her of Dak.

"Brave talk, Toby. You may reconsider when you see the bodies piled high. Your great-grandfather did."

No one said anything. The decision was Aldrea's. Had to be hers. "We go. But I warn you, Arn: You will not betray the Hork-Bajir and live. Now, let us go home."

<She calls it home,> Ax muttered.

Aldrea jerked my head toward him. <The Andalite,> she said silently to me. <What is an Andalite doing here?>

<He's a friend,> I said.

<My people were friends to the Hork-Bajir, too,> she said. Then she looked directly at Ax and, out loud, using my voice, said, "This human, Cassie, tells me you are a friend, Andalite. I warned her about Andalite friends."

<Did you warn her about Andalite *nothlits,* daughters of Seerow, who pretend to be Hork-Bajir?> Ax shot back.

<I am Hork-Bajir!>

<No. The Hork-Bajir are like Jara and Ket and the rest. You could perhaps consider yourself the equivalent of a Hork-Bajir seer, but your intelligence is not the result of a genetic fluctuation. I do not know you, Aldrea-Iskillion-Falan, but I know of you. You are highly intelligent, emotion-

ally self-controlled, capable of lying and manipulation for your own ends. You are also fundamentally peaceful, moral, courageous, and capable of self-sacrifice. You are, in short, an Andalite. Not a Hork-Bajir.>

"You could have been describing a human," Rachel said brightly. "Now, add in 'arrogant' and 'humorless,' and then you have an Andalite."

To my surprise Aldrea laughed out loud. My laugh. "Obviously you humans have spent some time with Andalites."

Ax didn't join in the sense of eased tension. He kept his large main eyes focused on me. On her.

<I want to be sure, daughter of Prince Seerow, that you realize you have only one function to perform. As soon as you show us the location of the weapons your *Ixcila* will be returned to storage. You are dead, Aldrea-Iskillion-Falan. When you have performed this one duty, this illusion of life will be ended and Cassie will be Cassie alone.>

The wall between me and Aldrea went back up. It felt even stronger than before. I had no idea what her true reaction to Ax's question was.

"I understand why the Ceremony of Rebirth was performed," she replied neutrally. "I understand that the Arn brought me here only to use me for this one purpose. I will do what I must."

Not the answer I wanted to hear.

<I will take back control of my speech centers now,> I said.

<Of course.>

A better answer. And if she'd given it without hesitation, it would have been better still.

CHAPTER 9

"Okay, we're supposed to brief you, so here goes: One of Cassie's best fighting morphs is a wolf," Rachel told Aldrea as we headed home through the sun-dappled woods.

The others had morphed and flown off ahead. At least they had been seen to fly off, and at least one no doubt did. There were plans to be made. We'd be away for a while. The Chee had to be contacted.

But if I knew Jake he'd left at least one or two others behind to watch us secretly. Jake was no happier with Aldrea's careful reply than I was.

This leisurely walk through the woods was a test. If Aldrea did anything troubling, Rachel was on hand, and probably Tobias and Ax, as well. I

didn't spot either of them. But I'd have bet anything they were close by.

Jake had suggested that Aldrea learn how to control my morphs. On the Hork-Bajir world, she'd be in charge. In a fight we needed quick responses. She needed to know which weapon to use. And we needed to see how she handled it.

"The wolf has good speed," Rachel chattered on. "Great ripping abilities with the teeth. Terrific endurance. They can run all night. Now if you'd chosen me, Aldrea, you'd have gotten some serious firepower. My African elephant morph. It's, like, fourteen thousand pounds. Not to mention my grizzly bear."

I felt a tickle of admiration mixed with amusement from Aldrea. A little of that wall between us had come back down, but what I saw and felt was only what Aldrea allowed me to see and feel.

I have to admit it's not as if I was pouring out my deepest, darkest secrets to her. I was controlling my body, my mouth, and my eyes again. But I was carefully not searching the trees and bushes for signs of Tobias or Ax, lest she figure out what I was up to.

"So, not that it bothers me, but why didn't you choose me, by the way?" Rachel burst out. "I mean, come on! There I was, all ready to go."

"Not that it bothers you," I said.

"Of course not. I'm just saying . . ."

<Why should I have chosen her?> Aldrea asked.

"She wants to know why she should have chosen you," I reported. "Should I explain to her that you are the mighty, the powerful, the ultimate Yeerk-killer, Xena: Warrior Princess, whereas I am merely an ambivalent, animal-loving, tree-hugging wuss?"

"You forget to mention that I clearly have a superior sense of style," Rachel added.

"Actually, I'm curious about why you chose me, too, Aldrea," I said, speaking out loud for Rachel's benefit. "We all thought you'd go for Rachel or Toby."

<I don't know,> Aldrea finally admitted. <I have no memory of making the choice. The first thing I was aware of was being in your body.>

Maybe it was because she'd been able to feel my admiration for what she had done by becoming Hork-Bajir.

No, that didn't make sense. I wasn't the only one who believed her decision to defy her own people to fight the Yeerks was heroic.

I relayed her answer to Rachel. I could have shared control of my mouth, perhaps, but it would have caused problems, confusion. I didn't want to give her any more than she needed. But

neither did I want to make her hostile by treating her with suspicion. *I don't think Miss Manners covers this particular social situation,* I thought.

<Aldrea, perhaps we could both access my speech centers. If we are each careful, we may avoid problems.>

"Yes," she said.

"Yes what?" Rachel asked.

"I-she-jamrff-coo har dabdiligg . . ." Two minds, one mouth.

Rachel gave us a fish eye. "Uh-huh. And meanwhile, back at the psych ward . . ."

<Go ahead, Aldrea,> I said.

"I thought I'd been given a ridiculous receptacle at first," Aldrea admitted, speaking to Rachel almost as if I weren't there to hear. "I didn't know how I would be able to fight in this soft little body. No blades of any kind. It doesn't even have hidden poison sacs!"

"Yeah, but she has an enema bag she uses on raccoons," Rachel joked.

"But now that I know it has morphing abilities, I'm sure it will work well enough," Aldrea continued.

It. I guess "it" is the right word to use when you're talking about a body. "It" stepped in to reach the speech centers.

"So, are you ready to try this?" I asked. "I'm

concentrating on my wolf DNA right now. Can you sense it?"

<Yes,> Aldrea answered.

"To start to morph all you need to do is —" I said.

<You're forgetting that I was born an Andalite,> Aldrea answered. <We invented the morphing technology.>

Her superior tone reminded me of Ax. Every once in a while he makes it clear how primitive our human technology still is.

I could have asked her how many times she'd morphed. How many animals. I could have pointed out that my friends and I were probably the galactic morphing champions. But I didn't feel right. I felt . . . I don't know. Aldrea was a hero right out of history. And I was the girl with the raccoon enema bag.

"Well, go ahead, then," I mumbled.

I felt the tip of my nose turn wet and cold. But only for an instant. My fingernails grew thicker and longer. But a second later they returned to their usual shape.

"You're fighting me, Cassie," Aldrea said.

"Oh. Sorry. I didn't know," I answered. "Go ahead."

I felt Aldrea begin to concentrate on the wolf DNA. I started to take a deep breath, then I real-

ized that right now she should be controlling the breathing. The changes began again. The bones in my legs cracked as the joints reversed direction. The skin on my arms itched as coarse hair popped through it. Morphing has always been creepy. This time it was terrifying. Each sensation felt magnified by a hundred. I wanted to scream as I felt my intestines shift and my ribs contract.

I ordered myself to get a grip. I decided to pretend I was watching a movie. I even tried to imagine I could feel the nubby material of the theater seat behind my back and the sticky floor under my feet.

When my lips began to stretch away from my face, I tried to think of it as a cool special effect in the *Aldrea: Alien Werewolf* movie.

It helped a little. Very little.

I fell forward on my hands. No, my paws. They were paws now. A moment later, the transformation was complete.

Aldrea took off running through the forest. I could feel her exhilaration. She felt powerful and free.

I felt as if I was locked in a speeding car with no brakes and no steering wheel. I tried to hold on to the image of the movie theater I'd created, but I couldn't. Not with Aldrea racing straight toward a huge pine tree! If we hit that tree at this speed there wouldn't just be a splash of fake movie blood. There would be an explosion of very real pain.

<Aldrea, look out!> I shouted.

She swerved, missing the tree by inches.

<What were you doing? You almost bashed my — our — head in,> I cried.

<What are you talking about?> Aldrea shot back. <This morph has excellent reflexes.>

She was right. I'd probably come that close to trees dozens of times when I was in wolf morph.

Aldrea was obviously having no problems controlling the body. I just had to trust her. Except she wasn't from Earth. What if a situation came up that she couldn't recognize? Would I be able to take over the body quickly enough to deal?

I decided to try a little experiment. Without saying anything to Aldrea, I tried to wag my — our — wolf tail.

It didn't move.

I tried again, concentrating all my energy on the muscles in the tail. The tail gave a twitch. It wasn't exactly a full-out wag. But at least it moved.

<What are you doing, Cassie?> Aldrea asked. She slowed from a run to a trot, and I got a little puff of annoyance from her.

I hesitated. I didn't want to admit I'd been trying to see what kind of control I had.

Rachel loped up beside us in her own wolf morph. I couldn't help thinking that if Rachel had been in my situation she would have gotten a lot more than a pathetic little twitch out of the tail.

Rachel would not have been intimidated by Aldrea. She'd have laid down the law: Do what I tell you, or else.

Or else what, though? That was the question, wasn't it. Or else . . . what?

I wondered again why Aldrea hadn't chosen Rachel as her receptacle. But maybe the answer was all too clear: Maybe I'd been chosen because she sensed that I was the weakest.

Had she felt that I would be the easiest to control? Had Aldrea, even in her inchoate *Ixcila* form, marked me as an easy victim?

CHAPTER 10

"Okay, there's that girl, Holly Perry, you know, she transferred from Polk?" Marco said from his seat on one of the big bales of hay in my barn. "I want my Chee to ask her out for me. I tried a couple of times, but this thing happened with my voice."

"He started clucking like the chicken he is," Rachel commented.

"Holly Perry. No problem," Erek the Chee told Marco. "It's not like we have anything else to do but work on your love life. Yeah, the Chee who plays you will also hold down his regular full-time job as a restaurant manager, but hey, your love life comes first."

Marco nodded. "Good. As long as we have our priorities clear."

Aldrea was completely lost. It was comforting to feel her confusion. <The Chee are androids,> I explained. <They can throw holograms around themselves to change their appearances. While we're gone, Erek's going to get a few of them to take our places at home and school. Passing as us.>

"If we're not back before the date, my Chee should just go out with her and make sure she really has fun," Marco continued.

"Do you think that's a good idea?" Rachel asked. "Won't Holly be disappointed when she goes out with the real you?"

I felt impatience from Aldrea. The emotional wall between us was becoming more of a sieve. Her thoughts were still beyond my reach, but I could "feel" her now as a person more inside me than out.

<It's their way of blowing off steam. You know, of dealing with the anxiety of leaving for a mission,> I explained to her.

Her impatience didn't lessen. <You are all still such children,> she muttered.

<Actually, we're not much younger than you and Dak Hamee were when you fought the Yeerks.>

I got the strong feeling that she didn't appreciate the comparison.

"Any other instructions?" Erek asked.

"Ask whoever is me not to be so nice to my sisters this time," Rachel answered. "They get to expecting it."

Erek smiled. "Jake? Cassie? Anything?"

Jake shook his head. I could tell that in his thoughts at least, he'd already left Earth far behind.

"Maybe I shouldn't ask this," I said slowly. "Maybe it's bad luck or something. But if we . . . if we don't come back, would . . ." I couldn't finish the sentence. A terrible grief welled up beneath my own less intense worry.

It took me a moment to realize that most of it was coming from Aldrea. My thoughts had made her think of her own parents and her little brother. All lost to her forever.

"We could stay with your families," Erek said. "If you really wish."

"No," I said quickly. "Forget it. No. I . . . I don't think I want anyone being me permanently."

Erek nodded. "No. I've lived a long, long time. Seen a lot of death. I've never seen the point in denying death. People die. People grieve. It's better than playing games with it." He turned to go.

"Oh, Erek, one more thing," Marco called after him. "I kind of need a makeup paper on some

great figure from American history. It's kind of due day after tomorrow."

"How about Franklin Roosevelt? I was the White House butler during his administration. I was the one who came up with the phrase 'New Deal.' Of course, it was during a poker game."

CHAPTER 11

For the second time in less than one full day, we were flying to the Hork-Bajir valley.

No one was talking. Marco and Rachel weren't bothering with their usual exchange of insults. Aldrea wasn't even communicating with me in our private shared-mind communication.

Jake wasn't saying much to me, either. He couldn't talk to me, even to reassure me, without talking to Aldrea, too. I knew he was aware of potential problems there.

I felt relieved when I spotted Quafijinivon, Toby, and the other Hork-Bajir already gathered around the small Yeerk spacecraft. It was larger than a Bug fighter, but still fairly small. Instead of the cockroach-shell shape with the twin ser-

rated Dracon cannon, it was closer to the oval shape the Andalites use, with an engine pod on either side. But the Dracon cannon were slung underneath rather than mimicking a raised tail.

I wanted to get on that ship as quickly as possible. The only way to complete this mission was to begin it. The only way to return to Earth was to leave it. The only way to regain the sole use of my body was to allow Aldrea to use it now.

I was ready. I had to be ready. That choice was made for me when Aldrea chose her receptacle.

I tucked my wings close to my body and let myself drop to the ground. I demorphed quickly.

"Anyone who doesn't have a Hork-Bajir morph, get one now," Jake instructed before the feathers had all disappeared from his face.

I stepped up to Jara Hamee and reached toward him. "May I?" I asked.

"Jara help," he answered.

I pressed my hands against his leathery chest. Aldrea fought to resist a renewed wave of grief. I couldn't figure out why for a minute, then I realized that touching Jara must remind her of how it felt to touch Dak Hamee.

It was all new to her. A loss that had occurred before I was born had happened to Aldrea just hours before. I couldn't stop thinking of it all as a story. Dak Hamee was history to me. To Aldrea he was a living, breathing person.

I acquired Jara's DNA as quickly as possible and slid my hands away. <You still really miss him, don't you?> I asked Aldrea.

<He died yesterday. And I was not with him. I did not hold his hand and tell him I loved him. Maybe in reality, but not in my memory, which is all the truth I have.>

<I'm sorry.> The words felt totally lame. But I didn't know what else to say. Aldrea said nothing more.

"It is time," Quafijinivon announced.

He took a step toward the ship, leading the way, then stopped and turned back to the expectant Hork-Bajir.

"Friend Hork-Bajir: I am deeply grateful for the gift of your DNA. I will do everything in my power to aid the new colony in banishing the Yeerks from your home planet. Believe me, or do not, but I tell you that I, the last of the Arn, will atone for the sins of my people."

Of course the Hork-Bajir didn't grasp half of this little speech. But they caught the tone.

Jara Hamee slapped his hand against his chest. "Free or dead!" he exclaimed.

"Free or dead!" Ket Halpak echoed. She slapped her hand against her own chest.

The other Hork-Bajir joined in the cry.

"Free or dead!"

Thump!

"Free or dead!"

Thump!

My eyes began to sting. I didn't know if it was my emotions or Aldrea's that caused the tears to form. In that moment our feelings were almost identical.

"Okay, let's go," Jake said.

Aldrea and I took one last look at the Hork-Bajir. We thumped our hand against our chest. "Free or dead!" we shouted.

"We" is the only way I can describe the experience. I'm really not sure if it was my voice or hers that uttered the Hork-Bajir battle cry. For that moment, the wall between us was down.

But as we made our way to the ship's door, I felt Aldrea pull away from me. I pulled away a little, too.

We were still almost strangers to each other. We both needed a little privacy. I stepped into the ship, Marco right behind me.

"Hey, all right. A hot tub," he exclaimed. "All you ladies are invited to join me." I followed his gaze to the small, drained Yeerk pool that dominated the only "room."

"It's empty," Quafijinivon reassured us. "I'll

take the helm. We will translate to Zero-space as soon as we clear the atmosphere. I must prepare for the trip to the Arn planet."

"The Hork-Bajir planet," Rachel muttered, with a significant look at me.

Quafijinivon didn't appear to hear her. He squatted uncomfortably, leaning back against a captain's chair designed for Hork-Bajir. The space beside him was without any chair, appropriate for a Taxxon.

Ax went to look over the controls. <This is a newer-generation Yeerk ship,> Ax commented. Then, his thought-speak tone elaborately casual, he said, <They've made some small innovations since they acquired the original Andalite technology from . . . well, we all know who gave the Yeerks the capacity for Z-space travel.>

"My father," Aldrea answered defiantly. "My father, Prince Seerow. Without my father, the Yeerks would never have had the opportunity to spread their evil," she continued. "Without my father, we would not all be risking our lives on this mission. That is the point the Andalite wishes to make."

<Aldrea, stop,> I begged. <No one blames you.>

She ignored me.

"All this is true," Aldrea insisted. "It is also

true that my father did what he believed was right. He believed he was helping a worthy race to advance."

<They advanced across the Hork-Bajir and now the humans.>

Aldrea whipped her — our — head toward him. "What he did is not so different from giving these humans the power to morph. And who did that, Aximili-Esgarrouth-Isthill? I know they could not have developed the technology on their own."

<You cannot compare your father to my brother,> Ax began to protest.

"Oh, but I can!" Aldrea cried triumphantly. "If your brother gave the humans the power to morph, that means he gave an inferior species technology they were incapable of developing themselves. That is all my father did."

"Wait a minute, are you comparing humans to Yeerks?" Rachel demanded. "Is that what I'm hearing?"

"Well, we're off to a good start," Marco said with a laugh. "We haven't even gotten to the first rest stop and already the kids are fighting in the backseat."

<You know, Ald —> Tobias began to say.

"Okay. Discussion over," Jake said. Tobias fell silent in mid-word. I could feel Aldrea's incredulity at being silenced by what she saw as an alien youth.

"We have to be a team here," Jake said in a voice so quiet it forced everyone to lean forward to listen. "We have to be able to count on each other. We're going deep into enemy territory. The Hork-Bajir planet is Yeerk-held. Ringed by Yeerk defenses. And we're relying on two people we don't know: Quafijinivon and Aldrea."

He shot me/Aldrea a hard look. "We'll be advised by Quafijinivon and Aldrea. And we'll always listen to Toby. But this is an Animorph mission."

"Meaning that *you* are in charge?" Aldrea demanded, almost laughing.

"That's exactly what I mean," Jake said.

I felt Aldrea's emotional reaction. A mix of resentment, condescension, and worry.

<Jake has led us through more missions, more battles than you and Dak ever fought,> I said, annoyed at her attitude.

Using my — our — mouth, Aldrea said, "I will follow Jake as though he were my prince."

Did she mean it? I couldn't tell.

I had the feeling Ax was about to say something snide. Jake raised his hand, cutting Ax off. "Thank you, Aldrea. It's an honor to have you on the team."

The moment passed. I saw Rachel smirking at me. No, at Aldrea.

<You care for this Jake person,> Aldrea said to me.

<Yeah. I do.>

<Like Dak and me.>

<Yeah. I guess so.> It was a disturbing comparison. Neither Dak nor Aldrea had survived their war.

<I wish you better luck than we had.>

<I'll open the observation panels,> Ax said. A moment later a ring of metal slid back, revealing windows in all directions.

My eyes went straight to the blue-and-white ball that was Earth. It was so far away already.

The ship picked up speed. It hurtled through space faster and faster.

Flash!

Earth disappeared.

<Translation into Zero-space,> Ax told us. <We should emerge somewhere in the galaxy of the Hork-Bajir planet. Depending on the current configuration of Zero-space.>

I looked around at our motley group. Four humans, a red-tailed hawk, an Andalite, a Hork-Bajir, an Arn with his back to us, and, invisible but still there, the hybrid thing called Aldrea.

I must have looked worried.

Marco caught my eye and laughed his sardonic laugh. "So. Yahtzee anyone?"

CHAPTER 12

ALDREA

I rolled over and realized that Dak was gone. I opened my eyes.

He was standing with his back to me. He was gazing out across the valley below. I stood up, started toward him, hesitated, then bent down to pick up the weapon I'd had within reach for every second of the last two years. I came up behind him, stepped around his curled-up tail, and put my arm around his waist.

We were at the edge of the small platform built seven hundred feet up in a crook of a Stoola tree's branches. We were at the far end of the valley, all the way down where it narrowed so much that the branches of trees across the valley reached and touched the branches from this side.

The Yeerks had searched the area thoroughly, hunting for surviving Hork-Bajir. The searching had been done by Hork-Bajir-Controllers. And yet we had escaped detection. Dak had taken the platform apart, buried it in the ground, then, when the search had passed, we defiantly rebuilt our little home.

"I love you, Dak."

He squeezed my arm against his chest. "Seerow is sleeping well now," he said.

"Yes. For the last few days, since the ships stopped arriving with all that noise."

A huge buildup had begun. The Yeerk forces, the forces we had fought, would be doubled.

"I fear for him, Aldrea."

I couldn't answer. My throat was choked. We had long since realized that we would not survive. We had accepted that. As well as anyone can accept the death of a loved one, or their own death.

But I could not accept it for Seerow, my son. Our son. Could not. And yet I could see no way out.

I looked to the little cradle of twigs where he lay.

"What will become of you, my sweet little one?"

He sat up. Too young to speak, and yet he

spoke. Not as a Hork-Bajir, but with fluency and ease.

"The Yeerks will take me, Mother."

"No."

"You will not save me, Mother."

"I . . . I couldn't."

"Where is Father?"

"What? He . . ." I reached, and Dak was no longer there. "He was just . . . what is happening?"

"Nightmare," the small, brown creature said. She had taken my son's place. "You're having a nightmare."

"Seerow!" I screamed.

The young Andalite sneered at me. <Did you imagine it was real, Aldrea-Iskillion-Falan? Did you think it could last?>

"Seerow! Dak! Come to me, come to me, let me . . . where are you?"

<Wake up! Wake up! Aldrea, wake up!>

"Seerow!"

I woke. Cassie, the human, had run to plunge our face into cold water.

I looked around, through her eyes. The lights had been darkened for sleep. The Andalite stood at rest, with a single stalk eye open, watching. Jake, the leader of the humans, had awakened.

"It's okay, Jake," Cassie said. "She just had a nightmare."

Seerow. Dead after a life as a Yeerk host. Dak. Dead, I knew not how. All of them, all our brave soldiers, all gone.

A nightmare. A dream of death from a person already dead.

CHAPTER 13

Three days had passed. Three days of having the strange, sad, secret Andalite-turned-Hork-Bajir in my head.

Sleeping with her on the hard, cold deck. Awakened shaking, sweating, wanting to tear my head open with my bare hands as I felt the awesome grief of her nightmares.

Eating with her, if you could call the concentrated nutrient pellets food. Going to the bathroom with her.

A lot more togetherness than I'd have preferred. Bad enough figuring out how to pee in a toilet designed for Hork-Bajir. Worse doing it with an audience in your own head.

We had gotten good at sharing control of speech. I controlled everything else. I had gotten used to it. I still didn't like it.

The Arn had stayed at the helm, ignoring us for the most part. I'd learned nothing more about him. Was this really some voyage of redemption for him? Aldrea doubted it. And she knew one hundred percent more about the Arn than I knew. Jake was talking with Quafijinivon when we translated out of the blank white nothingness of Zero-space into what now seemed to be the warm, welcoming black star field.

The Arn checked his sensors.

"Quafijinivon says we are now in Hork-Bajir space. We may pass the Yeerk defenses unnoticed. Or not," Jake announced. "We should get ready. We don't know what we'll be walking into. I want everyone —"

Marco held up his hand like he was asking a question.

"Yes, Marco."

"Do we have correct change for the tolls?"

Jake blinked. Then he grinned. He and Marco have been best friends forever. Marco knows how to knock Jake down a peg when Jake starts taking his fearless leader role too seriously.

Jake sat down on the floor across from me/Aldrea.

"I don't see why we couldn't have gone Z-space the whole way," Marco whined.

Ax and Aldrea both laughed. Then they realized they were both laughing at the same thing and they both stopped laughing.

"Just say it," Marco told them. "I am but a poor Earth man, unable to understand the ways of the superior Andalite beings."

"Hork-Bajir," Aldrea corrected him.

<Aldrea, why do you —> Ax began.

A flash of green streaked by.

"Shredder fire!" Aldrea yelled, and suddenly I was up and running toward the front of the ship. She had taken control of my body! It was so sudden, so effortless.

Ax reached the "bridge" first. He leaned his torso forward and looked over Quafijinivon's shoulder.

<One of ours,> Ax said. Then he clarified. <An Andalite fighter. It must be on a deep patrol. Harassing the Yeerk defenses.>

"Can we outrun him?" Jake demanded.

"They're between us and the Arn planet," Quafijinivon answered. "We're smaller. It's possible we could outmaneuver them. But it would place us well within their firing range."

Tseeeeeew!

The Andalite fired again. A miss! But the

cold, hard data from the computer made it clear exactly how close it had come.

"Fire back!" Rachel burst out. "Knock out one of his engines or something. Enough to keep him busy until we can land. They can't follow us down."

Quafijinivon's red mouth pursed thoughtfully. "Young human, that pilot is an Andalite warrior. One of the best trained fighters in the galaxy. I cannot hope to win a battle with him."

Ax and Aldrea both said roughly the same thing, which translated to human vernacular was, <You've got that right.>

<We can't fire on an Andalite,> Tobias said. He was flapping a little nervously, being tossed around as the Arn swung the ship into an evasive maneuver.

"So we let him shoot us down?" Rachel demanded. "There's one of him, eight of us. Or nine."

The Andalite fighter was coming back around in a tight, swift arc. In a few seconds his weapons would come to bear on us.

"Ax?" Jake asked.

<I cannot fire on a fellow Andalite who is merely doing his duty. Do not ask me,> Ax pleaded. <Maybe I could communicate —>

"No!" Aldrea interrupted. "If the Yeerks pick up a voice transmission, we're dead. They'll vector everything they have at us. We'll all be killed and so will the Andalites."

"Here he comes," Toby said.

I looked — and my stomach rolled over.

The Andalite fighter was on us. Seconds from firing.

This time he wouldn't miss.

CHAPTER 14

Ax leaped. He dragged the willing Arn out of the way and grabbed the controls.

<Computer, lateral thrusters, left side, full burn!> Ax cried.

WHAM!

I flew back into Toby. We both crashed to the ground. One of her blades nicked my arm and I felt a trickle of warm blood.

Everyone who'd been standing was pinned against the left side of the ship. An invisible force pushed me, forced the air out of my lungs, squeegeed my cheeks back against my ears.

Tseeeeew! Tseeeeeew!

The Andalite fighter fired.

A jolt of electricity, my hair tingled, Rachel's hair was standing straight out from her head, a blond halo. The air crackled blue. Then Rachel's hair dropped back into place.

The acceleration stopped instantly. I'd been straining forward and now, released, I tripped and fell like someone who's been tugging on a rope that snaps.

Marco landed sprawled all over me. He put his finger to his lips. "Shhh, don't tell Jake. You know how jealous he is."

<Left main engine down,> Ax reported. <And now he is angry. He is coming in slow.>

"Slow, that's good, right?" I said. I put my hand to my lip and saw blood on my fingers. I didn't even remember hitting anything.

"No, not good," Aldrea said. "He's decided we won't or can't shoot. He's coming in slow to make sure of his shot."

<Cutting lights, environmental and artificial gravity so I can give all power to the remaining engine,> Ax said.

The cabin went dark except for the glow from the control panel. And then I realized my feet were no longer glued to the floor.

"Ax, can we outmaneuver him? Yes or no?" Jake asked.

<No, Prince Jake, we cannot. But I cannot —>

Jake ignored his answer. "Aldrea?"

She knew what he was asking. I felt her ambivalence. Her hesitation.

"Yes or no!" Jake snapped.

"Yes," she said. She seized control of my body again, pushed off from the ceiling and floated weightlessly in beside Ax.

"Cripple him if you can. If not . . ." Jake said.

<Prince Jake, we cannot —> Ax pleaded.

"My decision, Ax-man," Jake said gently. "Aldrea, it's your show."

Aldrea wrapped a restraining strap over our shoulder to keep from floating away. My hands moved, taking a large, ornately designed joystick obviously constructed to accommodate Hork-Bajir fingers or Taxxon pincers. Aldrea's eyes, my eyes, were glued not to the slowly growing image of the Andalite fighter, but to the tactical weapons readout.

"Computer, go to manual firing mode," my voice said.

I watched the crosshairs on the screen swing across the field of stars and come to rest on the Andalite ship. Dead on the cockpit.

<If you were not in my friend Cassie my tail blade would be at your throat now,> Ax said in thought-speak only Aldrea and I could hear. <Do not miss.>

Aldrea moved my fingers again, ever so slightly,

gently, caressing the targeting crosshairs till they centered on the Andalite's right-side engine pod.

Had she retargeted because of Ax's threat? Or had she always intended to aim for the engine? In either case, a miss would likely mean a direct hit on the Andalite ship itself.

HMMMMMMMM . . .

TSEEEEEEW!

A single shot. The red Dracon beam punched through the blackness. Stabbed at the Andalite ship. Then a pale, orange explosion. The engine pod blew apart. The Andalite ship spun wildly, falling away from us.

"Yes!" Rachel cried as she drifted in midair, almost upside down. "You clipped an engine!"

<Targets approaching!> Ax yelled. <Multiple . . . I count four!> He swung his stalk eyes backward to look at Jake. <Yeerk Bug fighters. They are coming to finish him off.>

"Can he fly?" Jake asked.

<Yes. He is regaining control. But he is as slow as we are, now. He will never outrun them.>

"They won't attack us," Marco remarked. "They see we fired on the Andalite. We're a bona fide Yeerk craft."

<How lucky for us,> Ax said acidly. <That warrior has bought us our passage.>

"We just keep flying, we're home free," Marco pointed out.

Quafijinivon said, "Yes, yes! Keep flying."

One by one we looked at Jake. "Nah, I don't think so," he said.

Marco smiled. "I had a premonition you'd say that."

"Ax? Aldrea? Four of them. If we fire on the Yeerks, will the Andalite figure it out? Will he join in?"

<Yes!> Ax said. <He is already wondering why we do not finish him off.>

"Okay," Jake said. "Wait. Wait till you can't possibly miss your first shot. Then, boom! Boom! Boom! Boom! Four shots. Hit or miss it'll confuse the Yeerks, scare the slime off them."

Four Bug fighters loomed up from the brilliant crescent of the planet below, racing around their orbit toward us, engines blazing.

The Andalite ship seemed to be drifting now, helpless.

"Is he really —" Marco asked.

"No," Aldrea said. "He's hurt but not that badly. He's playing dead to draw the Yeerks in. He'll take one last shot. That's his plan. One shot and then die."

It was Tobias, the instinctual flier who saw the possibilities. <Hey, we drift left, get behind the Andalite, the Yeerks may hesitate to shoot, thinking we're friendly and they might hit us. They'll split left and right to get a safe angle of attack.

At that speed, that angle, you hit the left-side leader and —>

"And the debris will shred the following ship!" Aldrea said enthusiastically.

Ax hit lateral positioning thrusters for just a second, then we drifted, seemingly without power.

The Yeerks saw us in their line of fire, split left and right, just as Tobias had . . .

TSEEEEEEW! TSEEEEEW!

We fired.

BOOOM!

The left-side lead Bug fighter blew apart.

Tseeeeew!

The Andalite fired. The right-side leader exploded.

The left-side leader plowed into his partner's debris. An engine erupted. Ripped loose, sliced open the entire back end of the Bug fighter, which spun, then BOOOM!

Three Bug fighters down in less than ten seconds.

The Andalite fired his one good engine and went after the remaining Yeerk. But not before giving a slight roll to his ship. A sort of wave.

<Good hunting, brother,> Ax said.

Everyone started cheering.

"Good shooting, Ax and Cassie!" Rachel crowed.

“Yes, good work,” Jake said much more quietly. “We may have just alerted the Yeerks, made things harder. So take five seconds to celebrate, then get ready to land. Be ready for battle morphs if needed.”

<Cassie, I believe I like your boyfriend,> Aldrea said.

CHAPTER 15

ALDREA

Down. Down through the clouds, through the atmosphere that made the hull scream. Down to my home. The planet I had never left, and yet now returned to.

"The Yeerk automated defenses appear to have accepted our codes," Quafijinivon said.

"That would be a good thing?" Rachel asked.

"If they did not accept our identification they would have targeted us with ground-based Dracon cannon. We have another threshold to cross when we enter the valley proper."

I hadn't seen it from space since I first arrived with my family. My father, in disgrace, but acting as though he didn't know that this was a dead-end, irrelevant assignment for an Andalite whose

name had become a derisive joke, a synonym for "fool."

With my mother, just happy to have new, unclassified species to study. With my brother, who felt our humiliation so much more deeply than me.

All dead, of course. I'd seen them die in the blistering Dracon beam attack from low-flying Yeerk Bug fighters.

It was not a beautiful planet, at least not to Andalite sensibilities. An Andalite sought instinctively for the vast expanses of open grass, the delicate pastel trees, the meandering rivers and streams.

But the Hork-Bajir planet was scarred by the impact of the asteroid or moonlet that had erased its former character. The surface was barren, cracked, and fissured. The cracks were miles wide and miles deep, with shockingly steep sides. Life on the planet existed now only in those valleys.

There the giant trees soared. There the Hork-Bajir had once lived in peaceful ignorance, praising Mother Sky and Father Deep, harvesting the bark, avoiding the monsters that guarded the depths of the valleys.

We skimmed the barrens and then, suddenly, dropped into the valley. Dak's valley. My valley.

I looked and was suddenly glad that Cassie

had control of my body. If she didn't, I may not have been able to remain standing.

The trees! The trees! So many gone. The valley walls had been scarred, stripped. The Yeerks had cut deep gashes into the valleys to make level spaces.

"You must remember that it has been years since you last saw your home," Quafijinivon told me.

But it wasn't the years that had ravaged the trees. It was the Yeerks. More than half of them, gone. Pieces of most of the others had been blasted away.

<I should have known . . . I should have expected . . .> I said to Cassie.

Even before I . . . before I died, some of the trees had been destroyed. But now it was as if the planet had been massacred. For the trees were the planet.

"We appear to have been accepted and registered by the inner-defense grid," Quafijinivon said, breathing a sigh. "This is fortunate. We pass within a hundred yards of Dracon cannon in the valley walls."

"I can't believe we haven't reached the ground yet," Jake said. "How tall are these trees?"

I knew he expected me to answer. But I couldn't.

"The largest are two thousand feet tall," Quafijinivon answered. "The trunks a hundred feet in diameter. They are a masterpiece of Arn bio-engineering."

<Aldrea, are you all right?> Cassie asked softly.

<Turn away,> I begged. I hated the weakness in my voice, but I couldn't bear to look anymore. <Turn our eyes away.>

She did. But then, she looked again. And I looked, too. Because even now, scarred and blasted, raped and despoiled, it was my home.

"Two minutes," Quafijinivon said. "We will land just above the vapor barrier, within the former range of the monsters we created to restrain Hork-Bajir curiosity."

I felt the tension rise in Cassie. This was all alien to her, of course. A strange world.

For me it was familiar, and yet not. I had, in my mind, never left. The years had not passed. The change seemed sudden, massive, shocking. The destruction of decades in the blink of an eye.

But it was Toby who interested me. This was her ancestral home. A place she had never seen, but that must, in some way, be part of the substructure of her Hork-Bajir mind.

She was staring out of the window with curiosity, even fascination. But Hork-Bajir faces show little emotion. What she felt, if anything, remained a mystery. We would be landing, soon, and I didn't even know my own mind. I did not trust the Arn. I did not like the Andalite, but trusted him to be what he was.

I didn't know the humans, not even the one whose brain I shared. The one named Jake had performed well.

But I did not know what was ahead. I knew only one thing: Whether the Arn was true to his word or plotting some betrayal, it didn't matter. I had seen what the future held for my adopted world. And all my doubt, my cynicism born of exhaustion, was wiped away.

I, who had never left, was back. And I would make the Yeerks pay. No matter the cost.

I sensed the human, Cassie, reading my emotions, listening for clues. I was being careless. I closed my mind to her and sealed off my emotions.

CHAPTER 16

I felt the ship gently touch down. I felt the wall inside me go up.

I couldn't blame Aldrea. If the situation were reversed, I don't think I'd want to witness all the ways Earth had been violated by war and then have some second person reading my first thoughts.

"We have made it," Quafijinivon said with some satisfaction. "We are home. I will open the hatch and —"

"Hold up," Jake said. "What's out there? Should we morph to Hork-Bajir?"

Quafijinivon shook his head. "We're just above the Arn valley, in the no-man's-land. The

Yeerks don't come here now that all the monsters are dead. And, of course, they think all the Arn are dead as well." He gave a sad, dusty-sounding laugh.

He led the way to the ship's exit bay. I couldn't help noticing that his legs were slightly unsteady.

When I stepped onto the ramp, I was struck by how bright it was outside. That's really all I noticed at first — the intensity of the light and the way the sky almost seemed to glow.

"I must start my work soon, or risk a degradation of the DNA I harvested," Quafijinivon said. "My lab is not far. Follow me."

He led the way across a gently angled space of scrub bushes and weeds that ended abruptly in a jaw-dropping cliff that went straight down seemingly forever.

"You may not be aware of this, but not all of us have wings," Rachel pointed out. "At least not at the moment."

"There are steps," Quafijinivon assured us without turning around.

I gingerly approached the drop-off and peered down. Straight down almost nothing could be seen. But across the narrow chasm I could see that the far side was carved with doorways, windows, archways, and walkways. They were cut di-

rectly into the stone. Sections had been blasted away by Dracon beams, perhaps long ago, but the Arn village was still beautiful.

Jake said, "Tobias?"

Tobias flapped his wings, took to the air, and soared out over the valley. He floated for several minutes, using his laser-focus hawk's eyes to look down and around. Then he swooped back.

<I don't see anything alive down there,> he reported. <Pity. It's a stunning place. It must have been something when it was all inhabited.>

"Yeah. It looks like those Anasazi cliff dwellings in New Mexico or wherever," Marco said.

Rachel gave him a look. "Since when do you even know the word 'Anasazi'?"

"I've told you guys before, every now and then I stay awake in class. Just for a change."

Quafijinivon led us down a narrow stone staircase. There was no guardrail.

<It's times like these I appreciate my wings,> Tobias said. <I'd be real careful. You fall off and you'll have a long time to think about it on the way down.>

Jake, Rachel, Tobias, Ax, Marco, and Toby started down the side of the cliff after Quafijinivon. I fell in at the end of their single-file line. I wasn't happy about it. I'm not crazy about walking on cliffs. But it's not like I had a choice.

I locked my eyes on my feet, watching them

as they moved from step to step. If Aldrea was feeling any fear, or any contempt of my fear, she wasn't letting me know about it. She'd sealed up the wall between us and every brick was still in place.

"What's that red and yellow gunk at the bottom?" Marco called. "It looks like it's moving."

"Oh, thank you, Marco," I muttered. "Right now I really need to be thinking about what's way, way, way down there."

"It is the core of the planet," Quafijinivon answered.

"The core," Rachel repeated. "You're talking core as in center?"

"Yes, of course," he answered. His tone made it clear that he thought she was a little on the slow side.

"So, it's like a volcano down there, with lava and everything," Marco said. "How hot is that lava? You know, in case we fell in?"

"You're not helping," I told him, without raising my eyes from my feet. "Really not."

<You do not have to worry about the lava, Cassie,> Ax comforted me.

"Thanks, Ax," I answered.

<If you fell, I believe you would be incinerated before you hit the actual magma,> he continued.

Sometimes I think hanging around Marco so

much has given Ax a totally twisted sense of humor. Very un-Andalite.

Quafijinivon turned at one of the arches. One by one, we followed him into a long, narrow room, almost a cave.

For the first time since we started down the side of the cliff, I raised my eyes from my feet. I watched as Quafijinivon pressed a small blue pad set in one wall.

An instant later the whole wall slid open. A row of long, clear cylinders and an elaborate computer console filled most of the room.

"It took me years to piece together all the equipment I needed for a new lab," Quafijinivon said. "The Yeerk raids destroyed almost everything."

"I've never heard of Yeerks using Arn hosts," Toby said. "I understood the Arn spared themselves that by altering their own physiology."

"True, Seer," the Arn said. "The Yeerks did not kill us in pursuit of hosts. It was a game. A sport. My people were exterminated, our culture destroyed, because the Yeerks enjoyed using us for target practice."

The Arn's voice held only an echo of a bitterness that must go very deep.

Then the strange creature shuffled away. "I have work to do."

CHAPTER 17

ALDREA

Home. Planet of the Hork-Bajir. My planet.

I was desperate to escape from the soft, slow human body and feel my true form again. I wanted to be Hork-Bajir.

"Okay, we aren't here to sightsee," Jake said. "We're here to retrieve the weapons Aldrea and Dak hid. We find them, we tell Quafijinivon where to pick them up, and he flies us all home."

"Toby is already home," I said.

Toby looked up sharply. The idea surprised her.

"This is your home world, Toby," I said.

<Toby wants to stay that will be her call,> the *nothlit* hawk said. <The rest of us, me, Ax, Jake,

Rachel, Marco, and Cassie? We're all going home.>

The emphasis on "all" would have been impossible to miss. The creature named Tobias was warning me.

And what, I wondered, *would you be able to do if I decide that Cassie stays here?* But I said nothing. The humans and the obnoxious Andalite were already suspicious of me. Paranoid. Aximili was more concerned about me than about the Yeerks.

I had no allies in this group. With the possible exception of Toby. She was, after all, my great-granddaughter.

<Aldrea, he's waiting for an answer.>

<What?>

<Jake asked you a question.>

"I'm sorry, I didn't hear you," I said aloud.

"Are you ready? You're our guide. Take us to the weapons. Let's get this moving."

"Yes, I'm ready," I said. I tried to cover the uncertainty I felt, tried to hide it from Cassie.

I did not know the location of the weapons. I remembered Dak and I and the others, the few who still gathered with us, taking the ship. But I must have hidden them after recording my *Ixcila.*

<You don't know where they are!> Cassie accused.

<Nonsense!>

<Oh, my God! You don't! I can feel it. I can tell you're lying.>

<I know where I planned to put them. I know where they must be.>

<We have to tell Jake.>

<No!>

She opened her mouth. "J — . . . unh . . . Ja . . ."

<Let me talk!>

I released my hold, shocked at my own behavior. I hadn't meant to stop her, hadn't meant to battle for control. A mistake; I'd had no time to think it through.

Everyone was staring at me. All but the Arn who was busy elsewhere.

<Don't ever do that again, Aldrea,> Cassie said.

<I —>

<Don't ever fight me for control again.> Then she opened our — her — mouth and said, "She doesn't know where the weapons are. Not for sure. She has an idea."

Andalite facial expressions are subtle. But I had been born an Andalite. I saw the triumph in Aximili's eyes. The sense that he had judged me correctly.

Human facial expressions were still strange to me. Jake's face showed nothing. It seemed to be deliberately void of expression.

"That's something we should have thought about before we took off," he said mildly.

<May I use your mouth to speak?> I asked Cassie.

<Go ahead.>

"I am confident I can find the weapons. I know where I would have hidden them. Where I intended to hide them."

"That's great," Marco snapped, "but there's a big difference between getting yourself killed for a 'definitely' as opposed to a 'possibly.'"

"No one will be in danger. I know the place. I know the trees."

Jake said, "No choice now. We're here. But, you, Aldrea, are no longer to be trusted. You're mad at the Andalites, mad at the Arn, and you don't treat humans as allies. I understand your anger. You're in a very strange reality right now. But we get in and out alive, that's what we do. So if you get in the way, make me doubt you again, we will put you down."

I bridled at the insult and the threat. "This is my world, human. My battle. Follow me, do as I say, and you will soon be able to scurry back to Earth."

Rachel said, "And you'll be back in Quafijinivon's bottle."

"That's right," I said.

Jake took a deep breath and then said, "We

want to avoid Earth morphs if we can. No point announcing ‘The Animorphs are here.’ We’ll travel as Hork-Bajir. All but Tobias. I want you in the air, man. But stay out of view if possible.”

<On my way,> the *nothlit* said. He spread his wings, flew along the ground for a while, then flapped up and away into the mist.

“Okay. Now we morph.”

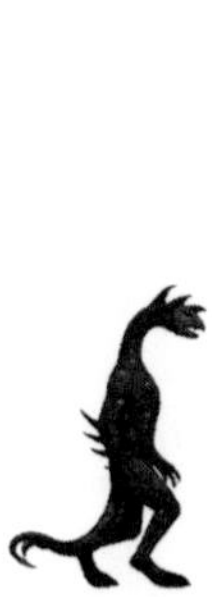

CHAPTER 18

ALDREA

<I assume you will control the morph,> I said to Cassie.

<Yes, I will,> she said.

I waited as she focused her mind on the Hork-Bajir DNA within her.

The changes began with surprising swiftness. Cassie was an experienced morpher, that much was clear. But as I watched the smooth, elegant transitions, I realized she was more than experienced. She was talented.

Her five-foot-tall frame expanded upward, growing like a sapling, shooting up by a full two feet. The muscles layered over her own weaker human musculature. The bones became dense.

The internal organs shifted with a liquid sound, some disappearing altogether, others appearing, forming, finding a place, making connections, beginning to secrete and digest and filter.

Her heel bone grew a spur, the Hork-Bajir back toe. Her own five human toes melted together, then split and grew into three long claws.

The tail grew as an extension of her spine, adding link upon link, bone growing from bone, wrapping itself in flesh and blood vessels and skin.

Her flat mouth pushed outward, lips stretching into a hideous grimace then softening into the familiar Hork-Bajir smile.

Then she did something I did not know could be done: She controlled the appearance of the blades so that they appeared, one by one, rippling up one arm, down the other, down a leg, up the next.

The horns grew the same way, one, two, three. She was showing off. Trying to impress me. And I was impressed.

<You have a talent for morphing,> I said.

<Thanks.>

I saw the subtle evolution from human to Hork-Bajir eyes. Colors shifted as the spectrum of visible light moved toward the ultraviolet, losing color toward the infrared end of the spectrum.

I saw the planet of the Hork-Bajir as a Hork-Bajir. I was truly home. Myself once more. Not a female, a male, but that was irrelevant.

I was Hork-Bajir!

All the others were completing their morphs. I was back with my adopted people. Or at least the illusion of my own people. And in my life as it was, at this moment, nothing could be free of illusion.

<Lead the way,> Jake said, obviously preferring to use thought-speak rather than struggle with the difficult Hork-Bajir diction.

<Cassie, I want . . . it would be best if I controlled this body, for now.>

<Okay. Do it.>

I pointed upward, out of the valley. "To the trees!"

We ran up the narrow stairs. Hork-Bajir did not fear heights. Up the stairs, across the barrens, feeling the slope grow ever more steep. Up through the mist. And then, still at a run, my head rose through the mist and saw the first tree.

Huge! It was a curved wall, a monstrous Stoola tree. My hearts leaped. I ran straight for it. Cassie ran. The Hork-Bajir ran. Andalite, human, Hork-Bajir all become one in the excitement of running, running, then leaping up, digging blades into the soft bark.

I was climbing. The experience that was so strange for an Andalite had been so strange for me for so long and was now so familiar.

To my surprise the human Cassie was both afraid of the growing height and, at a deeper level, strangely comfortable racing up toward the lowest branches a hundred feet or more up the trunk.

Of course. I should have realized: the arms that hinge through three hundred and sixty degrees, the strong hands with opposable thumbs, the feet with vestigial fingers.

<You humans are a brachiating species?> I asked.

<Of course. Our ancestors, the species that came before humans evolved, lived in the trees.>

<I felt that you were more at peace than an Andalite would have been.>

<Yeah, as long as we don't fall.>

<Hork-Bajir do not fall from the trees.>

Up and up, toes and blades biting the bark, racing straight toward "Father Sky."

<These are some seriously big trees,> Marco said. <This one tree could be lawn furniture for the entire country.>

<Why are we climbing?> Rachel asked. <I mean, we want to go somewhere, right? Not just straight up?>

<This is the way to travel here,> I reassured them. <Go up to go left or right.>

<I've been telling them that for a long time,> Tobias remarked. <Altitude is everything.>

<How's it look, Tobias?> Jake asked.

<I don't see any Hork-Bajir, or anything else except some small, fuzzy, monkey-looking things.>

<Chadoo,> I said.

<Whatever. Aside from that I just see some really, really large trees. I mean, these trees are up in my face. I don't mind flying through branches for a while, but I'm used to the air above two hundred feet being wide-open.>

We reached a long branch that ran almost level toward the south. Toward the valley's end where Dak and I lived. Had lived. Had given birth to Seerow.

If I had hidden weapons, it would be there.

And it was my home. A week ago, to my mind, it had been home.

I had to see it.

CHAPTER 19

Run!

We raced along the branch. Ran at full speed on a curved, uneven, knotted branch.

Ran like giant squirrels, sure-footed, and yet, within a few inches of falling and falling and . . .

The end of the branch!

<Aldrea, the branch is — AAAAAHHHH!>

Leap! Fly! Falling, arms outstretched, falling, wind whipping by, a flash of Tobias, leaves the size of circus tents.

She stuck out a hand. Grabbed a thin branch, I could close my hand around it, too small to hold us, oh God, we were going to die.

Falling, the branch bending down and down

and down and then, slower, slower, uh-oh, uh-oh, we were going back up! Spring action now whipped us up at dizzying, insane speeds, a giant rubber band, a slingshot, and at the top of the arc, she released.

<Aaaahhhhhh!>

We flew, somersaulted, and fell, down, down, THUNK!

My Hork-Bajir feet bit into a new branch, a new tree.

<Okay, that was nuts!> I yelled. <Let's do it again!>

The others were following, move for move, more or less.

We took off again, more businesslike now, but still swinging wildly from branch to branch, tree to tree in a trapeze act like no one on Earth had ever seen.

Aldrea stopped finally and rested. She watched the others catch up. More specifically, she watched Toby. The young Hork-Bajir seer was blazing through the trees, smiling, laughing.

<She's all I have left,> Aldrea said.

<You must have relatives,> I said. <Andalite relatives.>

<She is all I have,> Aldrea insisted. <And I don't even have her. I have oblivion.>

I felt a chill. Aldrea was right. This person,

this Andalite or Hork-Bajir, whatever she was who shared space in my brain, had nothing. She was not alive. Not truly alive.

Unless . . .

Unless she refused to return to oblivion.

It occurred to me then, for the first time, that Aldrea could live, through me, if I permitted it.

No! No, this wasn't up to me. Was it?

She was alive, now. Alive in a way. She spoke and thought and felt and experienced and even learned. She was alive, but only by my grace.

Oh, my God. Was it my decision to make? Would I have to tell her when the time had come to return to nothingness?

Was I going to be the one to kill Aldrea-Iskillion-Falan?

The realization took my breath away. Aldrea felt my emotions.

<What is the matter?> she asked.

I couldn't answer. What could I say? If I'd realized before I accepted the *Ixcila* I'd never have agreed to go along. It was impossible. It was immoral. Aldrea was alive, and if she died again, if she ceased to exist, it would come from my own selfishness.

There it was, I thought, the fatal weakness that had drawn Aldrea's *Ixcila* to me. At some subrational, instinctive level, Aldrea's spirit had

sensed the weakness in me. She had known that I could not, would not, demand her death.

Tobias came swooping past. <Aldrea, how much further in this direction?> he asked.

<Another quarter mile, no more,> she said. <There is a place where the valley grows so narrow that the trees reach across it and touch each other.>

<Not anymore there isn't,> Tobias said. Then, to Jake, he said, <Trouble ahead, fearless leader.>

<What's up?>

<You'll see for yourself in a few minutes,> Tobias said grimly. <Just keep your heads down.>

CHAPTER 20

ALDREA

Hearts in my throat I raced through the trees. All familiar, a path I had traveled a hundred times, a thousand, with Dak beside me, with Seerow hanging onto my belly as we moved.

Home. It was just ahead. Home.

And somehow, somehow, he would be there, Dak, strong, smiling, holding his arms open for me.

My son, my little one, my Seerow, he would be there in his nest, waiting, smiling happily to see his mother.

Impossible. I knew. I was not insane. I knew. And yet, the hope . . . irrational hope. An emotion not touched by all that I thought I knew.

Home!

I swung faster and faster, leaving the others behind, with only the hawk for company, now.

I stopped. A clearing where there couldn't be a clearing. An open space between the branches ahead. Sky rather than leaves.

No. It couldn't be. I would die rather than see it. No.

I crept forward and now the others caught up. They stayed back, cautious, knowing something terrible had happened.

At last I did not need to go closer. I saw. A hundred trees, gone. The earth was scarred, bare. A huge, open space, naked beneath the sun.

The Yeerks had destroyed most of the valley's end. It had been dammed up. A muddy gray sludge filled a crudely constructed lake. Tree trunks formed the sides. Bisected branches formed the piers that extended out into the lake.

Only it was not a lake.

My home, my valley's end where the branches reached across the chasm to touch, was a Yeerk pool.

The others caught up to me. We all stood amid the high branches and gazed down at the devastation. The humans did not understand, of course, not really. This was my home. Not from decades ago, but from just the other day. Just the other day I left my husband and my son there. Just the other day they were alive.

<I'm sorry, Aldrea,> Cassie said.

It was true. I was dead. I saw, I heard, I touched and felt, and yet, I was dead.

This life was no life at all. This life was an illusion created by the Arn. My life was Dak. My life was Seerow. Everyone who had made up my life with theirs was gone.

I looked for any last clue to what had been. These had been trees I knew. Trees that had personalities, at least to me. They didn't have the near-sentience of some Andalite tree species, but they were individuals nevertheless.

Stoola, Nawin, Siff trees, all gone, most burned away by Dracon blasts. Those that remained had been used to form the dam. Four of them laid lengthwise, stacked, then buttressed by saplings.

Behind the dam a billion gallons of the sludge Yeerks love. I knew Yeerk pools. I had spent my youth on the Yeerk home world with my parents. This had to be one of the largest Yeerk pools in existence. It might be home to ten thousand Yeerks, even more.

Then I spotted something I knew. Barely visible from this range. A minuscule patch where the

bark had been cut away. Nothing unusual: where there are Hork-Bajir, there is scarred bark.

<Friend hawk,> I called. <I understand your sight is very powerful.>

<Better than human,> Tobias answered. <Better than Andalite or Hork-Bajir, too.>

I told him where to look. And he described what I'd known he would see: The wood where the bark had been scraped away was cut with symbolic branches entwined. A bit of Hork-Bajir graffiti. A love letter.

<The Hork-Bajir symbol for undying love,> Toby told the others. <It sounds as if it contains the Andalite letters "A" and "D," as well.>

<The weapons will be there,> I said firmly. <Inside that tree. It has a hollow base. Dak and our fellow fighters used it as a hideout. There is a chamber inside, all smooth wood, silent and dark. The chamber is forty feet, almost round. Large enough to conceal a small transport ship. We cut a wide entry, disguised, grown over with new bark after each use.>

<You said you were not sure where the weapons are,> the Andalite said.

<I said I knew where we had most likely hidden them. That is the place.>

<It is part of the dam. It will be heavily guarded. Seven of us? It would be suicide, and for what? To learn that you made a mistake?>

<We mess with that tree,> Marco said, <the whole dam may come crashing down.>

<That's what she wants,> Rachel said. <Revenge.>

I said nothing.

<The entry you talked about, can you get it to open again?> Jake asked.

<Yes. It will still work. It was precisely constructed. And the water pressure will have kept it shut.>

<Water pressure?>

<Yes. The opening is on the far side of the tree. It is beneath the surface of the Yeerk pool.>

CHAPTER 21

It was not an easy plan to work out. We needed to get into the Yeerk pool itself. We needed to be able to function underwater. Aldrea needed to be in Hork-Bajir morph in order to open the tree.

Then, if she opened it, we needed to be able to get inside, enter the ship, and figure out how to fly it out of the middle of a log a hundred feet in diameter.

The plan we hatched was pure insanity. I knew this, not because Marco pronounced it insane, he thinks everything is insane. But I knew we were in trouble when Aldrea said it was insane.

"You have a better plan?" Rachel demanded. "Because we're all ears, here."

"What you are proposing is suicide!" Aldrea argued, speaking through me.

Marco laughed. "You've got my vote."

"We need a whale," Jake said. He looked at me, at Rachel.

"I'll do it," Rachel said. "Hey, it'll be —"

"No," I interrupted. "A sperm whale has a very narrow mouth. And I'm better at controlling a morph. Faster."

Rachel argued. Jake hung his head. He'd known it had to be me. I snuck my hand into his and he squeezed it briefly.

"This is not how morphing powers are used," Aldrea said. "Let's take our time, raid the Yeerks, take weapons, perhaps capture some Hork-Bajir and starve the Yeerks out of them, then, when we have an army —"

<You and Dak Hamee, all over again?> Ax said.

"I want this attack to succeed!" Aldrea shouted. "I don't want a wasted, futile effort. You humans are just children! What do you know about fighting the Yeerks?"

"They know quite a bit, Great-grandmother," Toby said.

Jake held up his hand, cutting off debate. "The Chee can't cover for us forever. We need to

get this done and get out of here. Aldrea, yes, it's crazy. But we've been doing 'crazy' since Ax's brother showed up."

There was a vote. Aldrea pleaded with me to vote against.

<I trust Jake,> I said. <If he thinks we can do it, we can do it.>

That's what I told her. What I felt was a whole different story.

<Cassie, don't be stupid,> Aldrea urged. <It is you who will die. The others will survive, but you will be the target.>

<I know.>

<If your timing is off by a few seconds . . . too much speed . . . too much mass too early . . . Cassie, you won't just kill yourself, I am in here, too! If you are killed . . . I won't have the option of returning to a bottle and awaiting some new chance at life.>

<I know that,> I said.

She was still arguing as I morphed to osprey. Still arguing as the others all morphed to flea or fly, all as small as they could get. Only Toby would not be coming along.

Once I was completely osprey, I picked the insects up, one by one. They crouched inside my beak. Not roomy or pleasant maybe, but safe enough.

I took to the air, released my grip on a high branch and floated out over the valley, out into the Hork-Bajir night. The narrow valley funneled heat upward, an almost continuous thermal that made flying easy. I turned in a spiral, flapped, rested, flapped again, higher and higher.

I flew up till I could see the barren lands beyond the chasm. There the thermal failed, dissipated by horizontal winds. I was as high as I could go.

<That's it, boys, girls, and etcetera,> I said. <I can see the Yeerk pool. The dam is brightly lit. There's a Bug fighter more or less hovering at the far end. Hork-Bajir are patrolling the dam, walking along the top. Both banks of the pool. They have guards everywhere. So. You guys need anything before I start?>

I was trying hard to sound nonchalant. I was scared to death. I was so far up, but not far enough.

<I could use a soda,> Marco said.

<We're not the problem, Cassie,> Jake said. <Just don't open your mouth and we'll be okay. We'll start demorphing as soon as there's room.>

<Okay.>

I took a deep breath. I picked my aiming point: near the dam, but not too near. I didn't

want to hit wood. I didn't want to hit as a full-fledged whale, either. A whale at that speed would be crushed by the impact.

Speed. It was all a question of speed.

I began to demorph.

CHAPTER 22

<It can't be done!> Aldrea warned.

<Yes, it can,> I said. <I can do it. Now please, shut up. I need to focus.>

I began to demorph. My talons became pudgy and grew into toes. My feathers melted together like wax under a blowtorch.

My face flattened, my beak softened into lips. My sensitive human tongue could feel the five insects inside my mouth.

Don't open your mouth, I reminded myself. But that was only my secondary worry. That part was easy.

The hard part was keeping my wings.

I fell. Down and down through the night. Down and down toward the bright Yeerk pool be-

low. Down toward the still-oblivious sentries who could burn me out of the air.

I fell, more and more human. But my wings, my osprey wings, I kept.

Morphing is never logical or rational. Things don't happen in a neat, predictable sequence. No one can ever be sure how it will happen. But I could, with some part of my mind I couldn't even feel, some part of my brain with which I could not even communicate, shape the way the morphing happened.

Ax says I have a talent. A gift. It wasn't my doing, and I don't know where it came from or why I have it. But, as I fell and demorphed and fell, my human body, my short, pudgy human body had wings that grew and grew and spread wider than osprey wings can spread.

I couldn't flap them or even turn the edges or control a single feather, but I could hold them stiff, and as I fell, I fell . . . slowly.

<You're doing it!> Aldrea cried. <Impossible!>

I fell slowly, reusing the accelerating pull of gravity. And then, only a hundred feet above the Yeerk pool, I began to morph to whale.

My feet twined together, like fast-acting ivy, or spaghetti twirled on a fork. They melted, and fused and my flesh grew thicker, fatter.

And still, I kept the wings.

Now I was within visual range of the Hork-Bajir guards. Now they could shoot at me, any moment, if only they looked up. One head raised to look at the stars and I would be —

Tseeeeeew!

A red beam appeared five feet from my face, then disappeared.

<Let go! Fall!> Aldrea cried.

<No! It's too early!>

<Jake, they're shooting!> I reported.

<Are we close enough?>

<I don't know!> I cried. <No. No, we're not.>

<Your call, Cassie. I trust you.>

Tseeeeew!

A second shot, this one behind me. More and more Hork-Bajir were looking up, goblin heads tilted back to see me.

They would not see a human. That was vital. We could not be here, certainly could not be humans. Humans on the Hork-Bajir home world? It would cause a galaxy-wide alert and bring more pressure than ever on Visser Three to find us, at all costs.

When the Hork-Bajir looked up they saw a melting, shifting thing with wide white wings and a whale's tail.

<Let go, I tell you!>

<Not yet,> I grated.

Tseeeeeew! Tseeeeeeew!

<Aaaarrrgghh!> A hole the size of a quarter appeared in my tail fin, smoking.

Tseeeeeew! Tseeeeew! Tseeeeew!

Red beams everywhere, left, right, some so near I smelled the air burning.

<I am taking over,> Aldrea cried. I felt her will surge, a tidal wave inside my mind.

<NO!>

She was trying to fold my wings, trying to drop, reaching to take over my mind.

Tseeeeeew! Tseeeeeew!

A shot burned a seven-inch slice into my side. The pain was staggering.

My wings were . . . closing . . . losing the morph . . .

NO! This was my body, this was me!

I shoved against the tidal wave of Aldrea's will, weak hands holding back a cataclysm.

But my wings stayed firm. I fell, faster, but not too fast. Aldrea fought me, I fought back, but I still owned this body, this morph. We fell, the strange, sad Andalite turned Hork-Bajir, the dead creature with a will of iron, and me. And all the while I morphed. Morphed till my osprey wings grew heavy with flesh that was as much whale as human.

The ground fire was a wall of flame.

At last, close enough. I demorphed my wings and plunged.

CHAPTER 23

ALDREA

I had lost.

We fell, fell toward certain death, plunged tail first into the Yeerk pool, and still, all I could think was that I had lost.

Lost to a human child. I'd assumed the only question was one of self-restraint. I'd believed I could seize this body if ever I chose. But the little human female had held me at bay even as she performed an act of morphing that would have made her a hero among the Andalites.

No time to think about that. No time to think about how she could have . . . no, there was a battle to fight.

We plunged deep in the Yeerk pool and now Cassie was growing with a shocking speed, grow-

ing so huge, so fast that the body was creating little whirlpools.

<Now I need you,> Cassie said.

I almost laughed. It was outrageous. Now she needed me?

<I am here,> I said. What else could I say?

<Use my eyes. Use my echolocation. Take us to the log and the opening.>

We swam, almost blinded by sudden, seething groups of Yeerks in their natural state. But the firing was done. The Hork-Bajir-Controllers could not fire on the pool. As the human Marco had predicted. Once in the pool we were safe. Until the Yeerks could evacuate their brothers, call them to the far end of the pool.

Then they would heat the water to steam with their Dracon beams and boil us alive.

Minutes. No more. Maybe less.

<I can't see,> I said.

<I'll fire echolocation clicks,> Cassie said. <You'll see a sort of sketchy picture. Relax into it. Let it happen to you, don't strain for it.>

She fired a series of rapid sonic hiccups. I read the picture. The sketch, really, as she had said.

<Left. A hundred yards. I think. I don't know.>

We were already moving, huge tail whipping the water, scattering lingering Yeerks.

In my vast mouth, the whale's mouth, Cassie's, I felt the others demorphing, growing.

<Need some air soon,> Jake said.

Cassie kicked, changed the angle of her fins, and skimmed the surface. <Whales don't breathe through their mouths,> she explained. <I'll need to travel on the surface, keep my mouth open.>

As soon as we surfaced, the firing began.

Tseeeeew! Tseeeeew!

Misses that caused eruptions of steam. And hits that caused agony.

<Diving!> Cassie warned. <Everyone breathe deep!>

And down we plunged, turned, and stopped. <Jake. We're there.>

<We're ready.>

Pah-loosh! Pah-loosh!

<I heard something,> Cassie said.

<Taxxons. They're sending Taxxons in after us.>

<Rachel and Jake will take care of them. De-morphing, now! Jake! Three . . . two . . .>

Cassie was confident that her two friends could stop a small army of Taxxons.

We raced toward the solid wooden wall ahead. We surged, dived, then suddenly rocketed up to the surface.

Into the air! Mouth wide-open. Amazing that this monstrous beast could almost fly!

<One!> Cassie cried. <Go! Go!>

Aximili and Tobias leaped. One real Andalite,

one morphed Andalite. Marco bounded, in Hork-Bajir morph. They landed atop the dike wall battlement.

We crashed back into the water, used our momentum to race along the wall toward where I'd heard the Taxxons. <Now!> Cassie yelled. She opened the whale's mouth again for Jake and Rachel.

<Jake, Aldrea says we have Taxxons,> she warned.

<Yeah, I can smell them,> Jake answered.

Jake and Rachel, a pair of streamlined, dark-gray aquatic creatures with sharply raked fins and a head that seemed squashed and flattened.

<Hammerhead sharks,> Cassie said.

Pah-loosh! Pah-loosh!

<More Taxxons!>

<It doesn't matter. Taxxon versus shark isn't even a battle, it'll be slaughter. None of the Taxxons will live to tell their masters anything.>

<You sound sad.>

<I'm worried for Jake and Rachel. It will be horrible for them.>

"Sreeeeee-yah!"

A Taxxon's scream resonated through the water.

<Worse for the Taxxons, from the sound of it,> I muttered.

<Okay, Aldrea, our turn.>

Cassie had already begun demorphing, building up the smaller, subtler changes so that she could finish in a rush. This part was critical. The humans were determined that the Yeerks never know they'd been on the Hork-Bajir planet.

And yet, Cassie had to be human, at least for a moment between morphs.

It happened quickly, but not instantaneously. We shrank, shriveled, wasted away at a shocking speed. Human arms and legs emerged from the vast tons of blubber.

Whale lungs became human, and Cassie kicked for the surface.

<They'll see you!> I warned.

<Have to breathe,> Cassie said. <Trust my friends.>

Her head, our head, broke the surface. Deep breath. Again. Battle just over our heads atop the dike wall. Two Andalites, tails whipping, slashing, cutting. Hork-Bajir-Controllers backing away and running as one of their own kept yelling "Run! Run! Andalites everywhere! Thousands of them, run!"

Marco, of course.

The Hork-Bajir guards broke and ran. None was interested in a human face poking up from the filthy muck of the pool.

Cassie steadied herself. I felt her exhaustion.

<You're tired.>

<Yeah.>

<It's a miracle you're alive!>

<Yeah.>

She began to morph. Hork-Bajir features appeared, but more slowly now. Too many morphs too quickly. And each a work of art.

As soon as the first blade appeared I said, <Cassie, slam the blade into the wood. It'll help keep you from sinking.>

I heard the sounds of Hork-Bajir-Controllers being rallied above, the shouts and threats of their sub-vissers.

The water echoed with the horrifying screeching of Taxxons.

<We are likely to be overrun within seconds,> Ax said calmly.

<He means, hurry!> Marco cried. <Hurry or we're toast!>

CHAPTER 24

I was fully Hork-Bajir now. I was done for. Tired inside and out.

<Take over, Aldrea,> I said.

Couldn't fight her. Needed her. My mind was going fuzzy, confused. Not sure what body I was in. Bits of unmorphed data, stray instincts, body images, echoes of fins and wings, all jumbled together.

Tseeeew! Tseeeew!

The battle above us on the battlements was joined again.

Aldrea propelled us down, crawling, Hork-Bajir style, down the dike wall, down into the water that no longer rang with the cries of dying Taxxons.

Two hammerhead sharks swam up beside us. There were bits of Taxxon flesh trailing from their rows of razor teeth.

Aldrea was running short of air. We were. She was searching in the murk for some sign on the vast tree trunk before us. Searching . . . the wood was swollen and discolored . . . gasping for breath.

<We're coming in!> Tobias yelled.

Pah-loosh! Pah-loosh! Pah-loosh!

Aldrea said, <Marco! Sink your blades into the wood, don't try to swim! Slow your heart-beats, it will preserve oxygen.>

There! The faint, almost invisible line. It was on the underside of the log, almost where it joined the tree beneath it.

Aldrea slashed with expert ease. Then she pulled.

Nothing!

<The water pressure!> she cried. <Too much. Can't do it!>

Marco crawled down beside us and added his strength.

Slowly the crack widened.

Tseeeeew! Tseeeew! Tseeeeew!

The troops on the battlement were firing into the water. They wouldn't be able to hit us, they couldn't even see us, but they'd soon parboil us.

WOOOOOSH!

The tree opened! Water rushed in, dragging us with it. A tangled mass of sharks, Andalites, and Hork-Bajir was swept inside and bobbed up, to my utter amazement, into air. There was no light, but there was definitely air.

It was silent inside the tree. All the sounds of battle were muffled.

Aldrea gasped, choked, breathed. Then, "Computer, identification: Aldrea-Iskillion-Falan. Code: . . ." She hesitated, then said, "Code: Mother loves Seerow. Ship, acknowledge by turning on exterior lights."

The sudden illumination seemed blinding after the total darkness.

We were floating in a placid pool at the bottom of what looked like an upturned, smooth, wooden bowl. We were inside the tree. Lying half-submerged in water was a stubby Yeerk ship, maybe forty feet long and almost as wide.

We paddled toward the ship and then I felt wood beneath my feet. We stood up.

Jake and Rachel were demorphing as fast as they could, and when they had feet and legs, they, too, stood up in waist-deep water.

"There it is," Aldrea said.

<You have no memory of this ship,> Ax pointed out. <How did you know the identification code?>

"The number represents a logarithm of Seerow's birth date. I always used it."

Jake clapped his hands briskly. "Okay, we have minutes before the Yeerks figure out we're in this tree. Let's get this over with."

We slogged over to the ship and hauled our wet, exhausted selves up inside. I lay on my back on the deck, unable to get up for a while.

"You okay, Cassie?" Rachel asked.

"Aldrea, actually. Cassie is exhausted," Aldrea said.

"Why are you in charge? Get Cassie back!"

Aldrea laughed. "You don't need to worry about Cassie. She takes care of herself quite well."

We stood up and went to the ship's controls. "I need someone on weapons," Aldrea said.

Ax appeared beside her. <We burn our way out?>

"We burn our way out."

<Once we create a hole, the water will rush in and through. It will create a vast drain that will empty much of the pool and suck many of the Yeerks to their doom.>

"Yes," Aldrea said. "Do you object, brother Andalite?"

<No, sister Hork-Bajir. I do not.>

"Then power up the Dracon beams."

The engines began to whine. The Dracon beams began to hum.

<You know, that says something that you can bury one of these things in a tree for years and then just crank her up like this,> Marco said. <Two points for Yeerk technology.>

<"Andalite technology,"> Ax and Aldrea said at the same instant.

"They stole it. That doesn't make it theirs," Aldrea added.

<Everyone should brace themselves,> Ax suggested. <There may be some instability.>

"Ready?"

<Ready.>

"Fire!"

The Dracon beams fired, a blinding blast. And kept firing. A hole burned through the outer side of the tree, out into the air. The water began to rise. The hole grew larger. Now the water was rushing in, gurgling up around the ship. The escaping air howled.

Then, all at once, the wooden wall was gone.

WHAM!

Aldrea hit the engines just as a wall of water caught us, slammed into us, and spit us out into the night.

The ship rolled, spun, bucked then . . .

Whooooom!

<Yeah! Yeah! Yeah!> Marco yelled. <Take that, George Lucas!>

The ship blew out of the log, down the valley, and turned to take a look back. A Bug fighter had come up, saw we were a Yeerk ship, and hesitated.

TSEEEEW! TSEEEEEW!

The Bug fighter blew apart and veered down into the draining Yeerk pool.

Water rushed out of the rapidly widening hole. I could not see the Yeerks, of course, but I knew they were being dragged along in the irresistible current. Hundreds. Thousands. We might never know.

I didn't want to know.

<I sense regret,> Aldrea said. <But this is a great victory. And it is because of you, Cassie. Without you, none of this would have been possible. You've just done the most impossible, incredible, and heroic thing I've ever seen.>

The water continued to drain. The Yeerks in host bodies might be able to save some of their brothers and sisters. Not many. Not all. Thousands of Yeerks would lie there, dying a slow death of dehydration as the water left them stranded, or asphyxiation as they sank, helpless, into the mud.

Because of me.

CHAPTER 25

ALDREA

We delivered the weapons to Quafijinivon. We were reunited with my great-granddaughter, Toby.

The humans, and the one Andalite, had done the impossible, the absurd! But there was no celebration. Instead there were awkward silences and stilted conversations and eyes averted.

I still had charge of Cassie's now-human body. She was doing something very much like sleeping. She had withdrawn, exhausted, depressed.

I drew Aximili aside. "You have lived with these humans. They seem troubled by their victory."

<Yes. They regret doing what they know they must. They have an almost Andalite sensibility.>

I smiled. "I was going to say that they remind me of our Hork-Bajir warriors, who never forgave themselves for learning to kill."

<Let us agree, then, that all civilized species must share a hatred of war,> Aximili said.

"It may be the definition of true civilization," I said. "And yet, we are here to promote another war. The Arn will spawn his new generation of Hork-Bajir, and, thanks to us, they will be armed."

<Young Toby will lead them,> the Andalite said, turning his stalk eyes toward my great-granddaughter.

Toby had her back to us. She had been working with the Arn, learning from him. A strange couple: the last remnant of the race that had made the Hork-Bajir to serve in simplicity and ignorance, and the living example of the Arns' failure.

She was so like Dak when I first met him. Before the battles. Before I had led Dak to serve the Andalite will.

"No," I said suddenly. "No, Toby will not lead them. Her place is with her people, on Earth. Someone, some part of Dak and Seerow and me, will survive to do something besides fighting a war."

<I do not believe she will go voluntarily,> Ax said. <She believes this is her duty.>

"No, I suppose that's true. But with your help, Aximili. And with Cassie's, I think I can convince her." I explained to Aximili. Cassie, of course, heard. And now, at last, she came up out of her haze of regret and guilt.

<You know what this means,> Cassie said.

<Yes. Yes, I know. But my life ended long ago. I tried to pretend otherwise. But with Dak gone, and my little Seerow, and even this planet that I loved so much . . . all that's left now is Toby.>

<No, Aldrea, that's not all that's left,> Cassie said. <You didn't stop the Yeerks. But you slowed them. And that gave humans time. Now we may not stop them, but we, too, will fight, and delay, and weaken them. And someday, somewhere, they will be stopped.>

<And one thing more,> she said. She turned our gaze to Toby. A young Hork-Bajir seer who would, at least in my last dreams, guide her people to freedom.

I almost weakened. It was so hard to say good-bye.

<Let's get it over with,> I said.

<It has been an honor, Aldrea. I still don't know why your *Ixcila* came to me, but it was an honor.>

<Don't you know? Even now? The *Ixcila* is drawn to a mind that reflects it. And I like to think even that inchoate, nonconscious version

of me was honorable enough to know I might be tempted. That I might be tempted to cling to life. And that I might need someone strong enough to return me to the path of my own fate.>

Cassie didn't say anything more. There wasn't anything to say, not to each other.

"Jake!" Cassie cried. "Aldrea is struggling to seize control of me!"

Jake and all the others jerked around, bristling, ready to fight.

Aximili moved quickly to get behind Toby. He whipped his tail forward and held the blade against the young Hork-Bajir's throat.

<Release your hold, Aldrea. You will leave Cassie's body or your great-granddaughter will leave her own.>

"Ax!" Jake cried.

"I'll kill you, Andalite!" I cried through Cassie's mouth. "The Arn will give me a new body and I will come after you!"

<I doubt that, Aldrea, daughter of Seerow the Fool. Toby will go with us as a hostage to ensure your good behavior in the future. Now. Leave our friend Cassie.>

I did. I left Cassie behind, lifted up out of her body, her mind, and was drawn back to the bottle.

I could no longer touch. No longer hear. No longer see.

For a while I could remember.

It wouldn't take Toby long to realize she'd been tricked. But by then Toby and the others would be on their way back to Earth.

My thoughts, my consciousness, my memory, were all fading. I still saw my son. Still saw Dak. Still saw . . .

Don't miss

ANIMORPHS®

#35 The Proposal

I haven't decided what I'm going to do when or if I survive this war and actually become an adult. But one thing I know for sure. It won't involve working in a restaurant.

As an Animorph, I've done lots of disgusting things. Heck, I've been lots of disgusting things. But I can tell you, nothing I've done before quite compared to emptying that pig bucket.

It only took a few minutes. But they were the grossest few minutes of my life. Shovels full of chicken bones, half-eaten hamburgers, slime-covered macaroni. All mushed together to make a cold stew more aromatic than a fly's wildest imaginings.

Oh yes. The life of a superhero is a glamorous one.

When I was finished, I raced back into the kitchen from the garbage alley. Waiters and waitresses surrounded the salad station. I squeezed through the throng, looking for the roach-infested, tomato-less salad.

Gone! It was gone!

"Hey," I cried to the salad guy. "What happened to William Roger Tennant's salad?"

He shrugged. "Gone."

"Did you tell the waiter the salad was for Tennant?"

"He can take the tomatoes off if he doesn't like them."

"Aaahhh!"

<Marco?> Jake called out from far away. <Is that you carrying us now?>

I squirmed through the crowd and bolted for the banquet room. Burst through the swinging door. Searched the banquet room for William Roger Tennant.

About twenty round tables covered with white cloths were arranged around the room. And at those tables sat people in tuxedos and fancy dresses and an unusually large number of overdressed girls my own age or younger.

That would be the Hanson fans.

Against the wall, to the left of the swinging kitchen doors, was a long, rectangular table, raised a few feet off the floor and covered with a long white tablecloth. The dais. Where the guests of honor sat. In the middle of the dais was the podium, from where William Roger Tennant would make his acceptance speech.

<Okay, Marco,> Jake said. <We're being set down now. We'll just have to hope we're where we need to be.>

I sprinted up the few steps of the raised platform. Three guests sat on each side of the podium. William Roger Tennant was seated to the immediate left of the podium. The podium blocked my view of his salad.

The three Hanson kids were to the right of the podium. I sidled up behind them, grinning and trying to look like I was supposed to be there.

<Marco,> Jake called out. <We're moving out.>

I reached Tennant just in time to see him lean over to the person on his left and say, "These tomatoes look delicious!"

"Aaaaahhhhhhhhh!"

The scream came from behind me.

<Uh, that doesn't sound like Tennant,> Tobias said.

<It sounds like Zac!> Cassie cried.

I spun around. Zac Hanson had fallen backward in his chair. His two brothers leaped to his aid.

"Aaaaahhhhhhhhh!" Zac screamed, frantically brushing at the cockroaches in his lap.

"Aaaaahhhhhhhhh!" a girl in the audience screamed back.

"Aaaaahhhhhhhhh!" Zac yelled.

"Aaaaahhhhhhhhh!" cried a woman in a long red dress.

"Aaaaahhhhhhhhh!" Within seconds, the room was filled with the sounds of women screaming, chairs overturning, men yelling "Sssshhhh!"

<Run! Outta here!> Jake yelled. Five cockroaches sprung from Zac Hanson's pants and fluttered toward the ground.

<Watch out for the feet!> Cassie cried.

"Aaaaahhhhhhhhh!" women and girls screamed.

<That horrible noise!> Ax cried. <Even with this insect's poor hearing I feel as if my head is going to explode!>

<It sounds just like a Hanson concert,> Tobias said.

A cockroach scurried by my foot. I snatched it.

<I have been captured!> Ax cried.

"It's me, man. I've got you," I whispered.

Four roaches shot out of sight beneath the long tablecloth.

<Who's here?> Jake asked. Rachel, Tobias, and Cassie all answered.

<Marco has me,> Ax said, crawling up my wrist.

<Ooookay,> Jake replied. <That could have gone better. Guess it's time for Plan B.>

<Some day when this is all over people will ask us about the war against the Yeerks,> Tobias said. <Let's leave this part out.>